FIGHTER

NYT & USA Bestselling Author
TIJAN

DEDICATION

I'd like to dedicate this to my readers, but also to Autumn Oertel.
She has shouted from the rooftops how much she's loved this story.
I'm honored to have her as a reader!

CHAPTER ONE

"Go, Dale!" my brother Dylan shouted in my ear. He raced from his side of the truck while I was still putting the engine in park. "*Come on!*" I heard him yell as he went past my door and veered to the back of the house.

I loved all nine of my brothers, but I was not one of them. For one thing, I'm a girl. My real name is Delia Holden. Our mom decided to give me the family name, but that's the most feminine thing about me. Delia had been shortened to Dele early on, and somehow that switched to Dale when I was in junior high. Which suited me fine. At that time, I liked fitting in with my brothers. I was scrawny enough to wear baggy shirts, baseball hats, and jeans with sneakers. People thought I was a boy, and I was athletic enough to play sports with most of the guys. That ended around eighth grade. My boobs came in, and my hips went out. Even though I was still thin, there was no way to hide my female lioness anymore.

I hated this, and watching Dylan sprint away, I cursed at him. That was the other part of being female that sucked: my speed had evaporated. I could no longer race and tackle him to the ground. I'd enjoyed holding my own against my brothers, but that had stopped, and by freshman year they were too cool to even be associated with me. They'd come around eventually as we all grew up, but things were never quite the same. Now here I was, home for the holidays from my first year at college, and I'd been roped back into the bounty-hunting business.

Our mom died from cancer when I was little, and our dad died when I was in high school. My mother had been sweet, quiet, and the perfect doting mom—a pile of crocheted doilies made for each kid testified to that fact. She really was perfect. Home-cooked meals, and she had picture books for each of us. I have memories of her waving goodbye from the window as the bus picked us up for school. However, our dad was the opposite. He was technically murdered in the back alley of a bar, but the real cause of his death was a lifetime of boozing, bar fights, and gambling gone wrong.

1

The social workers tried to take us into the system, but Dean was already nineteen then. He refused and instead got a job at a local bounty-hunting firm. Fast forward ten years and he owned the business. Every one of our brothers now worked as agents. The only black sheep in the family was me. I went to college, and it was moments like this that I was glad. No six a.m. busts. No accidentally Maceing myself. No worrying if my Taser had the lock on it.

I cursed under my breath, scrambling to tuck the keys into my pants and zip up the pocket as I tried to hold my gun so it wasn't pointed at anyone. Honestly. I'd been gone for five months. Five months of normalcy. Five months of staying up late to eat pizza and drink beer. Five months of going on dates. Five months of doing what other college students did, and I would bet money my friends weren't home chasing after a bail jumper. Oh, no. They weren't worried about whether they'd remembered to grab their handcuffs or not.

"*Dale!*"

Another brother waited at the other end of the house. He waved me over. As I ran to him, already feeling short of breath, he gestured to the south corner. "Radio when you get there."

Radio?

Shit. I forgot my damn radio. I glanced at him. Would he have an extra? Did I dare ask and risk being chewed out? Judging by the firm set of his jaw, I decided no. My cousins and brothers were nuts when it came to this stuff. If you forgot a piece of equipment, you got scrub duty at the end of the night.

I ran around to the backyard and saw Dylan in the opposite corner of the yard. He was looking all around with a hand to his radio. I heard him say, "South right side clear."

My cousin added, "Left front clear."

The rest checked in, and I heard Dean, my oldest brother, yelling from the front. "Where is he? We know he's here!"

"Dale!" Dylan waved his arms. He cupped his hands around his mouth and yelled, "Check in! What's wrong with you?"

What was wrong with me? Oh, the fact that they woke me at up six in the morning might've had something to do with it. Or that I hadn't worked out since I got on the airplane heading from California to Chicago back in August. Or the fact that I didn't want to do this, and they'd just assumed I would jump at the chance. I wanted to scream back at him and give him the middle finger, but instead I did my job: scan the windows, look for anyone looking back, look for any movement in the curtains. Look for pretty much anything. When I saw nothing, I yelled back at him, "I'm clear."

He lifted his radio and waved it at me. "Check in."

Across his radio, I heard, "Dale, check in. Check in, Dale."

I had no fucking radio.

"Dale!"

That was it. I gave him the middle finger this time.

He groaned in frustration, but checked in for me. "South left side clear." He paused, then added, "Dale's an asshole."

I lifted my finger higher above my head.

He laughed, but then our drama was forgotten. We heard Dean's voice from the front side of the house: "I don't care what rights you think you have. We have a warrant, motherfucker. Let us in. Now!"

I grinned, shaking my head. Memories of my childhood rolled back over me, and I adjusted my stance, leaning most of my weight on my left leg as I got comfortable. My job was to watch and report anything. My brother Dean's job was to roust the bail jumper, and as he continued to yell at whoever had been unlucky enough to answer the door, he was doing it to perfection.

I waved at Dylan and cupped my hands around my mouth to yell at him, "Who's the jumper?"

His hands immediately shot up in the air. "You didn't read the file?"

I'd been focused on dressing, coffee, brushing my teeth, coffee, finding my shoes, coffee, and then fixing my hair. They were lucky I remembered to grab a bulletproof vest. I shrugged.

A litany of curse words left him. "Are you kidding me?!"

I waited. He'd break. He'd tell me, acting like he was super disappointed. But I knew Dylan. He'd forget about this the instant we actually got the guy. Anyway I still had my fingers crossed, hoping the radio incident wouldn't be remembered later. I could grab a radio back at the office...hopefully before anyone remembered to confront me about it.

He swore again, but shouted back, "Your ex."

My what? I looked back at the house. Not recognizing it, I asked "Which one?"

Then a curtain moved, and I saw him. *Holy fucking hell.*

Dylan yelled, "Jaxon," but he didn't need to. I stared right into the piercing brown eyes of the one ex-boyfriend I'd hoped to never see again in my life.

Shit!

His brown hair was shaved into a crew cut, but it made him even more mouth-wateringly attractive. As I watched him look around, saw how the shadows played across his chiseled cheekbones and those perfect lips, knew I could testify to exactly how they could be used. I thought the fucker went to New York to pursue a modeling career. What was he doing back And why was he the bail jumper? Well…okay. I wasn't that surprised by that last part.

Then he saw me too, and I felt whiplash from the sting. His eyes narrowed. He stood there shirtless, his lean physique perfectly molded and sculpted. A smirk appeared, and I could read his thoughts. He was thinking of running for it.

My groin ached already. Jaxon was the guy I'd had to quit. For real. had to *quit* him. He was an addiction, and he got me into trouble, rather than keeping me out of it. My brothers hated him, but oh god…my eyes trailed down his chest again, and I remembered all the reasons I'd stopped listening to them.

He leaned back, brought up his foot, and my hand went to grab my radio. It grabbed my shoulder instead. *Crap.* This was why I should've swallowed my pride and asked for an extra. He was really going to run and Dylan was looking the other way.

"No!" I yelled.

Jaxon flashed me a grin. Good lord, he was gorgeous. He flung himself out the window, and I stopped admiring his perfect dimples.

I looked to see if Dylan had heard me. He hadn't. His ear was pressed to his radio, and I heard buzz coming from the other side of the house Then he took off, disappearing around the side.

"Dylan!"

He didn't stop.

Jaxon had landed in a roll and was up on his feet. He looked like a damn cat. The athleticism in one of his pinkies equaled all of mine (even in good shape) and half my brothers'. We were screwed.

He dashed past me and laughed. "Looks like you're going to have to tackle me, Doily. It's just you and me." He didn't wait around, though. He turned and soared into the woods behind the house.

For a moment, just one moment, I was mesmerized by the image of his ass. He wore black cargo pants, and they molded to his backside. It'd been too long since I had some of that fun. Then I remembered what I was supposed to be doing, and I tore after him.

I screamed over my shoulder, *"Runner!"* I wasn't holding my breath for help, and, gritting my teeth, I really was going to try to get him, just for the enjoyment of tackling him underneath me one more time.

Five minutes later, I realized I had no shot of getting him. My lungs protested, threatening to shut off completely if I didn't slow down, and my legs weren't helping. It was like they'd forgotten how to run. I almost pitched to the side twice, and my knees wanted to buckle, but in the end a log was my demise. I was running, or still trying—I was wheezing so loud that if I'd had a radio, I wouldn't have been to talk into it—when I saw the log. I jumped over it and was airborne when I saw the second log.

I screamed as my foot hit the log and my ankle went one way while I went the other. I crumpled to the ground.

Searing pain flared all over me, making my insides feel like they were burning up. I clutched my ankle and pressed down. My brothers always said to stop the swelling. I'd never read the bounty-hunting first aid manual to understand why swelling was bad, but I held my ankle like it was a life preserver. As I bit my lip and rocked back and forth, the rest of me tried not to let loose the water works. I was a girl, but fuck, I couldn't act like a girl. No crying, or I'd hear about this moment twenty years from now.

"Doily."

I glanced up. Jaxon had come back. He'd stopped a few feet away and watched me warily. Sweat ran down his chest, and he rested his hands on his hips. His pants slipped down, showing the V his muscles formed as they dipped beneath his waistband. As he knelt, his stomach muscles clenched even more tightly together.

I wanted to scream again. He looked so damn beautiful, and here I was. Sweaty. I felt my face and looked at the blood on my fingers. My hair was probably a mess, and I wore a pink tank top underneath my vest. It would've been hot, if the bottom wasn't disintegrated into shattered ends. Looking down at my jeans, I saw a big hole had ripped, and horror filled me as I followed the rip from beginning to end. Yep. It began at my knee and ended at my crotch.

Jaxon hadn't knelt to look at my ankle. He was staring right at my bright orange thong underwear.

"Stop." I groaned. Bending down so my forehead pressed to my leg, I thought maybe he'd go away.

His low, smooth chuckle rippled over me, sending old sensations and tingles through me too. He stood and came closer. Stopping so he was out of reach, he asked, "No radio, huh?"

I snarled at him, "Go away."

"You're supposed to trick me into getting close. Then you put those handcuffs on me. Remember?" He nudged my leg with his foot. It was a gentle touch, but I gasped. This hurt.

He bent down so he could actually look at my ankle this time. "That's how we used to have fun, remember? Hmmm…it doesn't look broken. Ice it and you'll be fine by tonight."

"What'd you do, anyways?"

His light, flirty look disappeared. He grew serious and stepped away again. "I can't tell you that, my little Doily."

I hated that name.

"And since you're not going to die, I'm going to complete my escape now."

"Jaxon." I looked at him, pleading now. "You can't leave me like this. Carry me back. They're probably still searching that house. They won't even think to come look for me."

He shrugged. "That's your problem. And they'll look for you."

At that second, we heard shouts behind us, and a wide grin came over his face. "See? You're the baby girl. They'll always look out for you."

"Jaxon, for real. What'd you do? I can help you." I needed to stall. Shoving the pain down and out of my mind, I focused on him. Bringing him in would prevent a lot of the teasing I knew I was otherwise going to endure. *Come closer, a little closer.* I started to wedge out my handcuffs from my waist and opened them. One quick flick of my wrist and I might be able to get them on his foot. Maybe. Using my fingers, and holding my arm in place to shield them, I started to slide the handcuffs wider.

He laughed. "I don't think so, sweet cheeks. Listen, I'll turn myself in after this weekend. I promise."

"Why not now? What's so important—" But even as I spoke, I knew. "Oh no."

He'd been watching me. As I connected the dots, his smirk grew. "Yeah. Sorry."

"You're fighting again?"

"I gotta make money somehow. I'm in the Boxing Day match this weekend."

I groaned, rolling my eyes. "We're not in Canada. We don't have Boxing Day."

He laughed, his top lip curved up in an adorable way, and began walking backward. He lifted a hand to wave. "Still. I'll see you this weekend. I'll even come to your bedroom so you can get the jump. How's that?"

He had a wicked glint in his eyes, but I knew he would follow through as promised. I also knew that meant we wouldn't be catching him until then. He was going underground, and we might not be able to find him until he was ready to be found.

"Dale!"

Dylan's voice came from back down the path. I looked over my shoulder, but he wasn't within view yet. "I'm here!" I yelled.

When I turned back, Jaxon was gone.

CHAPTER
TWO

I sat on the couch with six bags of ice all around my ankle. I only needed one, but nope, my brothers thought it was hilarious to make the pile as high as it could be. Dylan wanted to see if he could get it all the way to the ceiling, but Dean yelled at him for using too many ice packs. However, when I tried removing them, they just laughed and brought them back. I'd managed to wedge a blanket between some of the ice packs so there was only one actually on my ankle. I used the other ice packs to hide the blanket, so it was a win-win. My brothers kept laughing at me, my leg stuck under a house of ice bags, but I was secretly laughing at them.

Dumb shits.

It was either this or be harassed because I went into the field without a radio. *Really.* I knew better. The only one who was actually angry at me was Dean, but he was pissed because I hadn't used my feminine wiles on Jaxon. But hello? It's Jaxon. He's not exactly dumb—not like my brothers.

That evening around nine, someone shouted, and four of my brothers sprinted past the door to the back of the house. When I heard the office door slam shut and car doors open, I pushed myself upright.

Dylan sprinted past, or tried to. He held a coffee cup, so he could only jog or it would spill.

"Hey!" I yelled.

He jerked, and the coffee spilled on his arm. He turned to me with a scowl. "What the eff, Dale? I have coffee here."

"I have a question here."

He growled at me and looked around. When evidently he didn't see what he wanted, he used the bottom of his shirt to wipe off some of the coffee. "Yeah? What do you want? You got me while I clean up. Then I'm out of here."

"Where's everyone going?"

"Oh." The growl left him, and he started laughing. "You were had, little sister."

"What're you talking about?"

"The Boxing Day fight. Your boy lied to you."

"He's not my boy, and how do you know?" I wasn't surprised to hear Jaxon had lied. That was another factor in our breakup.

"We got a tip. He's fighting tonight, not on Boxing Day—although he could be fighting then too. But yeah." He finished cleaning up the coffee and frowned at his flannel shirt. Putting his coffee cup on the counter, he decided the shirt had to go. He tossed it on a chair and pulled off his white tee shirt, which had absorbed most of the coffee.

"Oh my," came a voice from the doorway.

There, holding onto the doorframe with her mouth formed in an O and her eyes traveling slowly down my brother's body, was my best friend. While I had straight, dark brown hair, Haley had blond curly hair. Almond eyes, tiny little lips, freckles sprinkled over her complexion—she was cute and gorgeous all at once. She had a small frame, boobs she wished were bigger, and slender hips, and she wasn't the only one drooling. Dylan's eyes were glued to her. No. Correction: they were glued to her rack.

I motioned to her. "Haley."

She didn't answer. She completed her first scan, arriving at his feet, and started back up.

"Haley."

She held a hand up. "Hold on. Girl's working here."

Realizing he was a fine specimen, my brother moved as if he were in slow motion. He started to reach for his flannel shirt, flexing his arm muscles, then turned his arm so his shoulder muscle bulged. The pectorals were next, and last, as he grabbed his shirt, he made sure to suck in his breath and twist to the side so his abdominal muscles were as cut as possible.

It could've been a scene out of a sitcom, as Haley wasn't even trying to hide her reaction. She held a latte in her hand, and while she drank in the sight of my brother, her hand lifted the lid. She let it fall to the floor as she dipped her fingers into the cup, then wiped them at the corner of her mouth.

She was foaming. I got it.

A second later, she glanced at me, biting down on her lip and trying to hold back her laughter. She pointed to herself. "Get it?"

I rolled my eyes. "He's my brother. You're disgusting."

Dylan realized his Magic Mike moment was over and chuckled buttoning up his flannel shirt at a faster pace. He gestured to the cup she was holding. "What's that?"

"A latte."

He narrowed his eyes and pressed his lips together. He started for her but she held it back and circled the room to me. "It's for your sister."

As she gave it me, I beamed. "Finally. The best friend has arrived."

She rolled her eyes, making a *tsk*ing sound, and perched at the side of the couch. Then she studied the mound of ice packs. "Uh, is that good for you?"

Dylan barked out a laugh, slapping his leg. "That's what she gets for not taking a radio out into the field."

Haley frowned at him. "What? She gets ice-packed to death?"

He stopped laughing. "What?"

"They said Jaxon is fighting tonight," I told Haley. "Do you know where?"

She looked back at me with an incredulous look.

"What?"

"Has college sucked all the intelligent cells out of you? It's Christmas Eve…" She waited, her eyebrows rising higher and higher. Then she made a circling motion in the air. "Come on…"

Christmas Eve. Fighting. Jaxon.

It hit me, and I fell back down against the couch. "Fuck me." Jaxon was fighting at Sally's, a hick bar known for their underground fighting matches. They always had a three-day tournament, starting Christmas Eve and ending on Boxing Day.

"Uh…" Haley tilted her head to the side. "I think he actually did that one time right there."

"What?" Dylan looked back and forth between us. He'd grabbed his coffee cup and now reached for mine.

I pulled it to my chest, shooting him a dark look. "Back off."

He rolled his eyes. "Whatever."

A honking came from outside, and he waved at them through the window. "I gotta go. See you later, and you'd better get all dressed and pretty. You're going to be seeing your boy later tonight." He gave us both a cocky smirk as he left, using his back to push open the door.

The second it closed, Haley turned to me. "Tell me you want to go too."

"Hell, yes."

We started knocking the ice packs off my leg. When she saw the blanket, Haley grinned and shook her head, but didn't say a word. When all of them were gone, she took one of my hands, and I pushed up from the couch with the other. Here was the testing moment: could I put weight on my leg or not? I would have to be able to walk.

Holding my breath and my latte, I started standing up. *Nope.* Daggers of pain shot up my leg, and I cried out. No way. I couldn't walk. "Great," I muttered. The pain almost made me drop my coffee. That would be a cold day in hell. Coffee came before everything. "Now what am I going to do?"

Haley thought, then her eyes lit up. She let go of my hand, and I barely caught myself as I fell back to the couch. I screamed at the sudden rush of more pain.

"Oh." She grimaced. "Sorry about that. But wait…" She ran upstairs, then downstairs, giving me a thumbs-up as she passed the living room. She threw open the basement door, and I heard her going down. She reappeared empty-handed and paused in the doorway to the living room. She scratched the top of her head, then her hand jerked up again. "I got it!" She sprinted back out through the kitchen, and I twisted around so I could see through the window. She was heading for the shed.

A second later, the big door for the shed opened, and she came back out, pushing my worst nightmare.

"Fuck me," I muttered.

She grinned brightly and waved her arms toward her find. "Voila. A wheelchair!"

Yep. This was my life. I was going to hunt down my ex-boyfriend in a wheelchair. This had to be a bounty hunter's most embarrassing moment. I mustered a weak smile and gave her a thumbs-up back.

She clapped and waved her hands in the air. "This will be fun! I want to wear a bulletproof vest."

CHAPTER
THREE

In the end, both of us wore bulletproof vests and sunglasses. As Haley pushed my wheelchair up to the handicapped entrance, my elbow rested on my lap, and my hand held my stun gun.

Yes. We were badass.

Then Haley tripped, and my wheelchair bumped into the rail, hitting my hand, and I dropped the stun gun in my lap. I froze, pure terror going through me, but it didn't go off. Haley stifled a scream as I turned and smacked her.

She yelped, cradling her arm. "Ouch."

"I could've stunned myself."

She nodded, and a laugh slipped from her lips. "Well, you're already in a wheelchair."

I glared at her. "We had another one in the shed." I raised the stun gun and pointed it at her.

She kept laughing and rolled her eyes. "Whatever. Be all menacing. I know you have a mushy heart, and besides, if you stunned me, who'd bring you coffee in the morning?"

I snorted. "You're not going to. What are you talking about?"

"That's true." Then, still laughing, she straightened the chair and started up the ramp again. Once we got to the door, we formed our own line. The other line of able-bodied patrons spread down the entrance and out onto the sidewalk. The ones waiting close enough to the door watched us the entire time. Some had their hands covering their mouths, laughing, but others glared. If we got in like this, I had no doubt they were going to rebel.

The bouncer turned to us, and I smiled, lifting my stun gun. "Let us in, Ace."

It was my cousin. He was large and in charge, and dressed all in black, except for the white lettering across his chest that said STAFF. Between his sunglasses, bald head, and tattoo circling his neck and trailing up the back of his skull, he would've terrified most people. Not me. He was just a year older than me, even though he looked thirty, and I had enough dirt on him to know he had a healthy fear of his mother. The knowledge I could share with her would be my blackmail.

"You have a weapon," he pointed out. "No way, Dale. Besides, your brothers are already here, and I have strict instructions not to let you in."

I pointed the stun gun at him. "Still have those strict instructions?"

He grumbled, but he knew I would do it. It didn't matter where we were or that my escape would've reminisced a tortoise trying to flee the scene.

He shook his head. "Fine. Whatever." He held open the door, and as we started in, he grumbled, "You got in through the back door, okay? Ted's back there, and he's wasted. If they ask him, he'll probably be convinced you actually did get in through there." He stopped talking as Haley brushed against his arm.

She smiled at him, slow and seductive. "Nice and large," she said as she dropped her gaze. "I wonder what else is nice and large."

He stood upright and fought not to smile back. Still wearing his shades, he scanned her up and down. "Still with that Carl guy, Haley?"

She tilted her head and trailed a hand down his chest. "We ended things last Friday."

"So you're living free and fun now?"

She winked at him. "How'd you know the names of my two girls?" She jiggled her chest, making her breasts sway. Then, continuing to laugh, she pushed my wheelchair forward. "Let me know if you've got some free time. I'll arrange an introduction."

He grunted, his eyes trained solely on her backside now. "Will do. Will do."

Once we were inside, I twisted around, frowning. "Who's Carl? I thought it was Clint."

"It was, but your cousin can call my ex any name he wants. I forgot how delicious he is."

"My cousin or my brother?"

"Oh." She pretended to swat at my head. "I'm single. Clint's been pretending he was single for the last two years, so I'm doing the same thing now. I have every intention of flirting with all hot male specimens who cross my path. Whether I hook up or not is up to me." She made a clicking sound from the corner of her mouth and winked at me. "Now, let's go find you some of your own fun and freedom, huh? Where's that hot piece of ass I know you're drooling to see fight again?"

I scowled at her, but I couldn't ignore the little burst of sensation that shot through me. A tingle of excitement. She was right. It'd been too long since I saw Jaxon fighting, and when she wheeled me around a group of people to an open space where we could see the fighting ring, I got a view that lit my groin on fire.

Holy. Shit.

Jaxon was already in the ring, clad only in black shorts that hung low over his slim hips. As his opponent swung at him, he dodged, and every muscle in his backside contracted, showcasing themselves for my viewing pleasure. Stepping forward, he twisted to the side and brought an uppercut, ramming underneath his opponent's chin. As he did, the rest of my lady parts jerked awake. I got a view of his front then, and his stomach muscles were just as ripped and sculpted as his backside. They were also red and bruised. He'd already taken a beating. I wasn't surprised. His opponent was twice his size.

Wearing a mean-looking scowl, his opponent stumbled back a few steps, then grabbed the rope to steady himself. The crowd was going nuts, and Jaxon didn't hesitate. He followed the larger man, delivering a series of jabs and uppercuts, from which his opponent couldn't recover. He fell to a knee, and Jaxon backed up, but he shifted on his feet, and I knew what was next: He sprang up, flicking his knee forward and bringing his foot down on top of the guy's head.

It was done after that. His opponent fell to the floor in a sprawl, and when the referee lifted his hand and let it go, it landed with a thump. He was out.

This was an automatic win, and the crowd roared in approval. Jaxon raked his taped hands over his face, spreading blood from his knuckles.

I also saw a cut at the top of his eye seeping blood. He might've made it worse, but he didn't seem to care. A cocky smirk covered his face as he turned to his corner. One of the guys waiting there helped him climb out of the ring.

"Again! Again!" The crowd started to chant, raising fisted hands in the air.

Jaxon lifted his head, his smirk growing, and turned back to the ring. His fallen opponent was being carried off, and another guy had jumped in. This one was leaner than the first but wore another ugly scowl. He began bouncing up and down, stretching his arms over his chest, and he waved a finger at Jaxon, beckoning him into the ring.

I recognized this guy. It was Downtown Sculley. He was known in the underground scene. I wheeled my chair forward and leaned closer to see the gleam appear in Jax's eyes. If he beat Downtown Sculley, his reputation would be cemented. It would up his credibility, and he could demand more money with each fight he won.

"No, no," I murmured to myself. I didn't know if Jax could win, and I didn't want to find out. He was awake and conscious. If he got knocked out, my brothers would get him and therefore get the skip money. Jax was *my* jump, more out of pride than anything else. I'd screwed up, so I needed to bring him in. I grabbed Haley's arm and yanked her down to me.

"Ouch!" She glared at me. "What?"

"He can't fight that guy."

"Why?" She glanced around. The crowd was still chanting because Jaxon hadn't climbed back into the ring yet. But I knew he would. "If he loses, we can grab him easier."

"No." I shook my head. "My brothers will grab him. We need to get him now."

"How?" She kept frowning. "I don't think he'll even see us—or hear us if we yell."

I bit on my lip. She was right. *Think, Dale, think!* How could I get his attention? As if answering my own question, the throbbing between my legs deepened, and I squirmed in the chair. I needed to decide whether I wanted his attention to take him to jail or because I needed some other release.

I gestured for Haley to bend down. "Where's the closest fire alarm?" I asked.

"Uh…" She scanned the room, which was filled with Christmas lights. A palm tree decorated with condoms and thongs stood in one corner, and mistletoe hung all over. A waitress walked by with her red shirt knotted underneath her breasts, and I noticed she had a necklace of mistletoe around her neck. She saw us, stopped, and frowned with one hand resting on her hip. She wore a very short pleated green skirt, and she cocked her head to the side.

I met her gaze. I knew she was wondering whether we should be here or not, so I smiled at her and lifted my stun gun. Her eyes went wide, and she hurried away.

Hayley groaned. "Why did you do that?"

That waitress had been eyeing Jaxon earlier. I shrugged. I should've hidden the gun, but I couldn't refrain. Seeing the fear in her eyes had been worth it.

"She's getting security."

"Well, that seals the deal," I said as I saw what we'd been looking for. I pointed to the fire alarm. "Go pull it."

Just then a guy turned around right in front of it, and we both stopped. It was my brother Dylan. He laughed, holding a beer in one hand and talking to a customer.

"Thought you guys didn't drink on the job." Haley said, eyeing him.

"We don't." But some of us did our own thing. *Hello.* In a wheelchair here. "Haley, you can still go over and pull it. Go to the side like you're going to the bathroom and slide behind him."

Dylan tipped his head back, taking a good sip from his beer, and his eyes fell on the ass of a girl in front of him. She danced to the music and looked over her shoulder, catching his eye. Giving him a shy smile, she slowed and moved closer.

"Oh, yeah. He definitely won't see you—" I began.

I stopped talking. It was pointless. Haley was already halfway across the room, but she wasn't hiding. Oh no. She swayed her hips from side to side, and it didn't take a genius to figure out she was trying to get Dylan's attention. When he saw her, his eyes widened, but then he frowned and started looking around for me. Haley blocked him. She lifted her arms, pretending to yawn, and as she did, her shirt raised an inch, and Dylan's eyes went right where she wanted them: to Fun and Free themselves. She had her back to me, but I could tell whatever she was doing was working. My brother looked entranced.

Stopping right in front of him, Haley hip checked the other girl and drew her finger along my brother's neck, moving up to the tip of his chin. She lifted his head, curling her other arm around his shoulder, and then— Was she really? Yep.—she pressed her lips to his.

I was shocked, but only slightly. Haley and Dylan had flirted for years. I waited to see if I should be disgusted. I felt a surge of joy when my brother grabbed her hip and pulled her close against him (not that part—that part was gross). Her arm lifted behind him, reaching for the fire alarm. As she deepened the kiss, her right hand wound around his head and grabbed his hair, then her left finger lifted the handle for the alarm and lingered on the lever.

I still needed to get in place. She was giving me time.

I didn't waste it. Sally's had three exits: one through the kitchen, a second back by the restrooms, and a third to the left, hidden behind the stage where the deejay had set up that night. Everyone would clamber for the restroom exit and the deejay exit. Knowing Jax, I figured he'd go through the kitchen. There would be the least resistance there since a lot of the customers didn't know about that one, so I started wheeling. I intended to block him and slap my handcuffs on him. I just had to get there first.

I wheeled past the main bar and was almost to the kitchen entrance. I ignored the attention I received and glanced back to where Haley was still kissing Dylan. *Oh whoa.* He had her pressed against the wall now, right beside the fire alarm. Both of her hands were twisted in his hair, but she was looking for me. Our gazes collided, and she shoved my brother away for a split second. Taking a deep breath, she pushed down the alarm and grabbed his hand.

The sound split through the air a second later, along with flashing lights from every alarm in the bar.

There was pandemonium after that. If the alarms were going off, that meant the fire station had been alerted, and that meant the police too. People pushed to get out. The underground fighting tournament wasn't a secret around our town, but as long as the cops didn't "officially" know where it was, they couldn't arrest anyone for attending. However, if they were actually called to its location, all bets were off. Hence the chaos.

When I saw a bunch of the staff running toward me and the kitchen exit, I pumped the wheels of my chair faster. I went through the door and parked by the counter. Jax would be running past me soon, and knowing a catch was coming had my adrenaline buzzing. I could barely stay sitting in the chair, even when people sprinted past and threw confused looks my way. Let 'em look. I had my handcuffs ready. I was going to get him. I knew it. Then he burst through the door and flew right past me.

"Well, fuck." I sighed. I hadn't counted on that happening. Putting my cuffs away, I started wheeling myself forward.

"Holy shit!" someone yelled behind me.

That was all the warning I had. I'd started to turn around when my wheelchair tipped over, and suddenly I was sprawled out onto the floor. Feeling the burn from the impact, a split second of terror went through me as, in slow motion, I saw the onslaught of people coming my way. They were going to stampede over me. I threw an arm forward, trying to grab hold of something to pull myself out the way, but then I was hauled into the air.

Jax tucked me against his chest. I glimpsed the firm set of his jaw and knew he was pissed, but he took off running with me. I looked down to find my handcuffs were gone. I peeked over his shoulder and saw someone kick them underneath the counters.

They'd be no help to me now, but hell, I was in his arms again. A girl couldn't be too picky. I'd figure something else out. I still had my stun gun.

CHAPTER
FOUR

After Jax set me back down on my feet outside, I cringed. My ankle still hurt. I grabbed onto his truck for balance and took a moment to focus on easing the shooting pains going up the inside of my thigh.

He used those thirty seconds. He was fast too. His hands skimmed over me, and before I could stop him, my stun gun, radio, and pepper spray had all been deposited in the back cab of his truck. He reached to pull the cover back down, but paused and studied me.

I knew what he was thinking. I had a second set of handcuffs stuffed down my pants. My jeans were tight enough to hold them in place, but he wouldn't...he would. I caught the speculative gleam in his eyes and then his gaze lingered on my waist. My shirt had ridden up, so he got a good eyeful of skin. I flushed and tried to tug my top down, but it was too late. He'd seen the slight bulge at the side of my hip. As he came toward me, I tried to position myself so he couldn't reach around. Maybe I could still grab them and work some magic... But he grabbed my wrist. A smirk on his face, he tugged me against him. My hip wasn't protected by the truck now; it was firmly in the palm of his hand.

I cursed in my head as my body came alive, pressing against him. It had a mind of its own. It was like something had turned off the control board in my brain. The *something* being all my lovely lady parts, which were panting for him. A fervor worked over me, and I had to be honest: I tried to think *no* and remind myself what I needed to do, but as his hand started to slide inside my waistband, that thought quickly faded. My body said *yes*.

A slow pant began building, and then he removed his hand and brandished my pink handcuffs in front of me. "I knew you kept a second pair."

I groaned, my head falling to his shoulder. "Jax, come on. Let me take you in. I'll post your bail tonight even."

"Nope." He still stood right in front of me, but reached around me to open his door. His chest rubbed tighter against me as he did this. I heard the locks unlock, and he swept me back up off my feet.

"Jax!"

He carried me around to the passenger door and deposited me inside. Seat-belting me in, he flashed me a heart-melting grin. "There you go. Good as gold, my sweet Doily."

"Please." My head fell back against the seat. "Don't call me that."

A low chuckle was my answer as he shut the door and hurried around to his side. People continued to stream out of the bar as he backed out. Looking in the rearview mirror, he said, "So tell me, was this your plan all along? To get me alone?"

"What are you talking about?"

He laughed again, but his eyes were intent on the crowd behind us, so I didn't think he was laughing at me. He shook his head and made a soft clicking sound. "I saw your brothers during the first fight. I was trying to figure out how to get out of there without running into any of them. Was that your plan? To help me escape?" He cast a look at my ankle. "The helpless invalid look threw me for a loop until I figured out you weren't acting. You really are helpless tonight. Not your usual look, Doily, but it's kinda turning me on." He turned onto the road and winked at me.

I sighed. *Shit.* My insides were turning all gooey, and I hated being gooey. I was tough. I was badass. He flashed me another grin as he turned onto a gravel road, and my heart leapt a little in my chest.

I was a screwed girl. Then I tuned in and realized he wasn't taking me home. Leaning forward, I started studying the road. When I saw Old Man Frampton's farm, I gasped. "What are you doing? Take me home."

"Nope."

"Jaxon." I frowned. He lived in the opposite direction, so he wasn't taking me to his place either.

He ignored me and kept driving. As he did, I studied him. I should've been paying attention to where we were going, but I knew how to get home from Old Man Frampton's farm, so I figured I could guess at directions when I called Haley to come and get me. Right now I took advantage of this

time while Jax was concentrating on the road. He was rarely sidetracked
He was usually a man on a mission, and most of the time that mission ha
been to get in my pants when we were together. He succeeded eight out o
ten times too—a fact he never boasted about, but I knew he was proud of

This time, though, he wasn't focused on me, so my eyes roamed al
over him, drinking in the sight. His black shorts rode low, and he hadn'
put a shirt on, so I could watch as his chest rose and fell, illuminating hi
lean build. Then I noticed the fresh bruises, and a pang went through me
Scooting closer so I could see better, I reached to touch one on his ribs, bu
he caught my hand.

"Easy there, city slicker," he drawled, looking down at me. Ther
wasn't much space separating us. "You'll get me all excited, and we'll b
having another impromptu picnic, midnight style."

I flushed at the reminder. There'd been another time when I'd scootec
close to him, started caressing him because he'd been hot, I'd been horny
and I'd had too much wine while I was waiting for him to pick me up
We never got to the restaurant and ended up eating old crackers after w
pulled off into a field to satisfy some of my more urgent needs. A nev
rush of excitement came over me. I'd missed these times with Jaxon. He
was unpredictable and delicious in so many ways, but I forced myself t
imagine a cold bucket of water raining over me. I needed to cool down.

Jump first. Think later. That's how life with Jaxon had been. I'd been
in too much trouble, and I'd fought hard to stay clear of all that at college
I couldn't start living life with that mantra again.

"Where are you taking me?" I murmured. "You know my brother
can track my phone." I slipped my hand inside my pocket. My pocket wa
empty. He'd grabbed it.

Jax just waited, the cocky smirk permanently etched on his face.

I jerked upright in my seat. "What'd you do with it?" I hit his arm
"That was an expensive phone."

"Relax, Doily. When I picked you up back at the bar, it fell out of you
pocket. I might've kicked it under a counter. No one will find it there." H
glanced at me sideways. "I'm assuming it was on silent?"

I groaned. "Yeah." He was right. If he kicked it far enough under
counter, it'd probably remain there until my brothers tracked it down

Sally's wasn't known for their cleanliness. It'd be safe from anyone sweeping underneath.

"Look, Doily—"

"Dale," I snapped.

"Doily—"

I gritted my teeth.

He kept going as if I'd never interrupted him, a slight chuckle in his voice. "I can't drop you off at your place. I'm not stupid. Your brothers will be there waiting for me, and there's no way I'm taking you back to my place. I'm sure they got that staked out too. I'll go in. I promise. You can take me yourself after my last fight, but I can't go to jail right now. If I do, that's an automatic disqualification to fight, and I have to win this tournament."

"Why?"

He glanced at me again. I could sense the hesitation.

My eyes narrowed. "Out with it, Jaxon. I can either help you avoid my brothers, or I can make your life hell. You pick. Tell me what's going on, why there's even a warrant out for you, and I might help."

He seemed to be holding his breath, then he let it out in a rush and muttered, "What the hell am I doing? Fuck it. Fine." He looked at me again, just as we drove under a light post. It slid shadows over his face, illuminating his cheekbones, and for a moment, it gave him a deadly presence. Then the shifting of darkness and light were gone, and I heard the old Jaxon start talking, but with a serious note to his voice.

Jax was rarely serious. The two times I'd seen it hadn't gone well. The first time he'd put someone in the hospital, and the second was when I ended things between us. I felt a little uneasy, but I pushed that away. I needed to concentrate on what he was about to tell me.

"There's a warrant for my arrest because I beat up my sister's boyfriend a while back," he said. "I was arrested, and I was supposed to go to a court hearing, but I couldn't that day because Libby decided to go missing. I had to search for her. I was scared she'd gone back to him."

"To her boyfriend?"

"Yeah." His jaw firmed. "The guy's an asshole, but she's infatuated with him. He's nothing but a sniveling little weasel, and he hit her."

I gasped. "Libby?"

He nodded. "I don't know what's wrong with her. She knows he's bad news, but she keeps going back. This has been going on for a while, but anyways, I found her that night. She was at Monroe's."

"What? Why?"

"Trust me. I wasn't happy either."

Monroe's was the closest thing our town had to organized crime. It was a candy shop, but the basement was where the real action occurred. There was an illegal casino, and if Libby was there, I didn't even want to think what that could mean.

"Her boyfriend's a weekly customer," Jax added. "He's worked up a good debt to them, and Libby was trying to pay it off. She was going to work there—"

"*No!*"

"I got there in time and promised I'd pay off his debt as long as they don't let him gamble there anymore."

"They agreed to that?"

"No." He shook his head, his shoulders lifting and settling back down as if they carried an unbearable weight. "They didn't agree to that. But they do want me to fight this weekend, and they promised that if I win, they'll never touch Libby. She won't work there. She won't even be allowed in Monroe's, and they won't use her to collect his debt. That's the best deal I could do."

"So you have to win the whole thing?"

"Yeah, and now do you see why I can't go to jail? Even if it's just for an hour, I can't risk it. I'll be disqualified. They'll know I went in. Someone there helps recruit fighters for the whole thing, so I'll be ratted out, and I can't risk it. This is too good of a deal, and Chris Monroe is an all-right guy."

I nodded. Chris had gone to school with us. He was head of the Monroe crime family now, but Jax was right. Chris had an honor about his criminal life. If he promised something, he'd follow through, and I'd never admitted this to Jax, but I'd always felt like Chris had a thing for Libby. Part of me wondered if he wouldn't protect Libby anyway, but it was too risky.

I knew why Jax was doing what he was doing, and with that, I let out a defeated breath.

Fuck. I was going to help him. I was probably going to jump him in the process, but I was going to help him keep fighting.

"Does that sound mean what I think it means?"

I looked at him, holding his gaze as he kept driving. The corner of his mouth curved up, and the cocky Jax was back in action. He winked at me before turning back to the road. "Thanks Doil—Dale. I mean it."

"I get to walk you in, though—on Sunday, after your last fight." That was my only condition.

"Sure. No problem." He flashed me a smile, one of those heart-stopping and bone-melting ones. "Thank you, Dale. It means a lot to me."

Well, it should, because I knew we'd have trouble ahead. My brothers were smart and savvy. They were already biting at the bit to get him, but because I was with him now, they'd be worse. I had no clue how to work it so Jax could get in and out of the next match without getting caught. But the other problem—like an annoying, pesky tickle at the base of my spine—was Jax himself. Somehow, in some way, I knew he'd get out of this unscathed, but I wouldn't. I never did when I spent too much time with him.

I had to help him, but I'd have to help myself too, and that meant keeping a cement wall around my heart.

Jax reached out and patted my leg. Just like that, one touch, and a frenzied need coursed through me. My body grew hot, and I squirmed, wanting that hand to go farther north.

Cement wall, Dale, I told myself. *Cement wall around the heart.* But as his finger caressed my leg, I already knew a cement wall around my whole body would've been pointless. It always had its own mind when it came to Jax Cutler.

CHAPTER
FIVE

He pulled onto a long and winding gravel road with trees on both sides. When his headlights flashed over them, I could see how thick the forest was. I wanted to ask again where we were going, but I knew Jax wouldn't tell me. He'd make a smart-ass comment because he didn't trust me—not fully, not yet.

After a curve in the road, an old house appeared. It was a two-story, and it should've been white, but it looked more gray and black from not being washed or painted in so long. Piles of newspapers sat in front of the door on the front porch. A chair and lawn chair were set up next to the papers, but as we drove to the garage in the back, I saw the spider webs covering them with a white film. I wrinkled my nose. I hate spiders. The urge to go over there and start wreaking havoc with a broom, hose, and shovel for all the newspapers had me gripping the door handle. I squeezed it and told myself to leave the spider webs alone. This wasn't my hideout.

Jax parked right before the garage and hopped out. He left my pepper spray, handcuffs, and stun gun in the truck and came around to my side. The door opened, and before I could say a word, he pulled me out of the truck and cradled me against his chest.

Well. His chest had cooled during the drive, and I pressed a hand against him, feeling his heart pick up its pace. This was lovely. I refused to look up. I could feel his eyes, and there was no way I was going to get pulled into his web. It could get sticky, and I'd probably not want to leave.

He carried me inside and set me on the kitchen counter before going back outside. I glanced around, but the room was still dark. I couldn't see much. Jaxon came back in with a bag over his shoulder, which he tossed to the side, then flicked the lights on. I looked around a cramped kitchen with dirty dishes in the sink. There were bread crumbs on the counter, and Jax scooped them off, letting them fall from his hand over the garbage. He flashed me a half-smile, going to the refrigerator. "You want a beer?"

"Tell me you don't live here." There were two couches in the living room, both covered by blankets to hide the cushions. But the blankets didn't cover the bottoms of the couches, and I could see the insides hanging out. Just looking around the place, I could feel my allergies kick into high. "Jax, if a piece of mold grew legs and scurried under this table, I wouldn't be surprised."

"It's not that bad." He grabbed two beers and handed one to me. Leaning back against the counter, he dipped his head back, taking a long swallow from his bottle. As he did, I looked away. A man shouldn't be that beautiful just taking a drink. "Besides, this is your fault," he added.

"Mine?"

He wiped the back of his hand over his mouth and pointed his bottle to me. "Yep. I had a better place to hide out today, but your brothers found me. Thanks to you, I was ousted. Besides, this is just for the weekend, and I needed a place where no one would find me." He spread his arms out. "Voila. Casa de Jaxon's Hideouto was birthed."

I made a throwing-up sound. "We can't stay here. Whose place is this?"

He shrugged. "I have no idea. I asked Lady G for a place I could hide, and she gave me this address."

"Lady G?" This went from worse to the *worst*, if that made sense. "You asked your grandmother? Is she in town?"

"Nah." He chuckled, taking another drink from his beer. "She's on some cruise, but she asked around. I told her it had to be low key."

"You told her about the warrant?"

He nodded. "And about Libby and the Monroes' promise."

Mold and dust came over me in waves. I was starting to struggle to breathe, and a headache had formed at the base of my skull. I shook my head to clear it. "Wait a minute. Let me get this straight...what about the money? If you win?"

He lifted a shoulder. "Chris said I could keep it. I'm assuming they're betting on me."

"Or they're going to have you throw it?"

"What?" He looked dumbfounded. "No fucking way that's happening. I fight. I win. That's what Jax Cutler does."

"And." My eyebrows shot up. "Follow the bouncing balls." Lifting my finger in the air, I pretended to point them out. "Dot, dot, dot. You're known for winning. That's your reputation. They told you to fight. They're going to get in touch with you right before the game and make you throw it. I bet you anything."

He snorted. "No way. I mean, yes, I love my sister, but I have *some* dignity. My reputation would be down the drain then."

There had to be a way to fix all of this. Then a light bulb went off, and I snapped my fingers in the air. "Do what they want."

"Throw it? Are you serious?" He gave me an incredulous look.

"Yes. Do it for Libby." I shot a finger up in the air. "*But,* challenge the winner afterward to another fight."

His eyebrows furrowed together. One of his hands lifted to rub at his jaw. "And Chris Monroe?"

"You did what he wanted, or what we're assuming he'll want. I mean hello? Chris is going to want to make money. Having you fight is a no brainer. You'll win. Everyone will be betting on you, but if you challenge the winner the next weekend, you could win back your reputation and maybe even some money."

"The pot was fifty thousand." He sounded wounded. "I'm going to lose out on *that* money."

"Jax." I snapped my fingers. "Libby." Did I need to say more?

He sighed and finished his beer. "I know." He tossed the bottle into the garbage, a clean shot, and reached for my beer. I hadn't drank from it, and he took it out of my hands. "Just let me have a minute," he added. "There's a man's ego at risk here. I'm going to have to take a beating."

"Literally." I flashed him a grin.

He nodded. "Exactly, but I'll be fine. I'll regroup. I'll slam the fucker back down, whoever beats me, and Libby will be safe. All is good."

"And I'll get to take you to jail that night."

"You're right. You win too."

"Uh-huh." My head bobbed up and down, but as we talked, darker sensations had begun to stir in me again. I felt the air grow thick with tension, and I was engulfed by nerves, excitement, lust—all that bang and buck together. It was like my body knew the talking was nearing an end and had started to remind me how much it wanted that man again.

Trying to stall for time to put that cement wall back in place, I glanced around again. "Can we go somewhere else?"

"Like where? Your brothers know me. I'm sure they have every place staked out."

Yeah. His places. I cursed under my breath. I should've thought of it sooner.

"What?"

"They're looking at *your* places. Not mine."

"Meaning?" Then the corners of his mouth dipped. "No way. I'm not shacking at Haley's. I've been there. No offense to your girl, but there's too much pink and lace. I need to be able to fight, Doily. My manliness will be sucked dry if I set foot in her doorway."

"No." My brother would be staking out that place, but in a whole other way. "My family's cabin. It's nice. It's not seasonal, so they won't even think of it being used. But its warm enough outside that we won't freeze." And it was clean. That was the more important factor. No allergies to clog up my lungs. "What do you think?"

"I don't know." But he was thinking about it. I could see that, and his eyes flicked over the place. He lifted a hand and scratched behind his ear. "I don't even want to know what boyfriend of Lady G's this place belongs to anyways."

Hope surged up my throat. "Yeah?"

"Yeah." He gave me a grin and stood in front of me. Bending down, he patted his back. "Hop on, Doily. Let's get out of here. It's giving me the creeps too."

I slid down, my good leg wrapping around his waist. He reached back and kept a secure hold under my injured leg, then moved outside and deposited me in his truck. Disappearing back inside, he was gone for a moment. Then he came back with a case of beer in one hand and his bag in the other.

He handed over his phone.

I asked, "What's this?"

"I just realized your brothers might think I've kidnapped you. I'd be in worse trouble then. Can you call them? Let them know this isn't that type of thing."

I lifted the phone and dialed my oldest brother Dean's number. I knew he'd scream and blame me somehow, but Jax was right. He didn't need another warrant, one that would ensure him some prison time.

"Dale?"

I let out a silent sigh, getting ready. My brother sounded pissed.

"Hey, um, you're not going to like this," I told him, "but I'm going to stay and talk Jaxon into going to jail…"

"Bullshit. Are you in bed with him already?" Dean argued. Then he was quiet for a moment. I could hear him breathing. "So you're saying you're going to help him?"

Well, the whole idea of not letting him know the plan had gone south. Not wanting Dean to think that I was a floozy (even though my loins cried at the injustice of being accused and not actually being in Jax's bed), I said without thinking, "I am not sleeping with him! I'm just helping." And immediately after, chaos ensued.

Dean started shouting. I shouted back. Curse words were thrown, along with a few threats, and eventually Dean delivered an ultimatum: "Tell us where you are right now or you're cut out of the holiday party," he said, sealing the deal for me.

Oh, hell no, my brother.

I'd been leaning against the truck's passenger door, but I jerked upright after that. Without pausing, I snapped back, "I may not like the holidays, but kicking me out of the family party isn't your call, Dean. But fine. Fuck it. See if I want to come anyway." I set my jaw and reared back, ready to throw the phone into the dashboard, but Jax swooped over. I flung it in the air and his hand snatched it, just a few inches from mine.

My eyes went wide at his quickness, and I crossed my arms over my chest. I wanted to pout. My brother was going to kick me out of the party— but damn, Jax's swiftness was seriously hot. I shot him a look. "I hope you know what you just cost me."

He smirked, his eyes sparking. "Your family's parties are always the same: Booze. People getting drunk. Boxing on the television, and everyone threatening to take out their Taser guns. You hate your family parties."

Shit. He was right. Still, it should be my decision whether or not to go. I leaned back against the truck. "I stir at the stove—that's my job—and I drink. Dylan always bitches, but he brings me a new beer every time he sees I'm out. And I stand there because I can listen to all of the conversations at once."

"You miss your family, huh?" Jax's voice softened.

I closed my eyes against that tone from him. *Shit, shit, shit.* It was enough to make my toes curl and little tingles shoot through me. The cement wall was crumbling again.

I looked over at him. "Because of the party? No. I'm being stupid. You're right. I usually hate them." The fighting. The loud voices. The bickering…which led to wrestling which led to laughter about how the wrestlers both sucked, and then the night would end around a bonfire. Stories being told. More laughter.

All of it was pure chaos, but Jax was right. I had missed my family— since we broke up. I sighed. I'd ended things and left two weeks later. I hadn't been back since.

Feeling my tongue swell at more of my stupidity, I waited to see if he would bring it up.

There was a moment of silence, and when he spoke, his voice sounded odd. "If we're going to devise a plan for how to get around your brothers tomorrow, we should get going. Your cabin is another twenty-minute ride, and I think we both could use some sleep."

And fuck me.

The caring and soft Jax just went away. I could feel a wall slam into place between us, and when he started the truck and pulled onto the road, I had a feeling neither of us would be getting much sleep tonight.

CHAPTER
SIX

And *I* didn't.

When we got to the cabin, there wasn't much conversation between us. The bed in the master bedroom was a king. Not sure about the sleeping arrangements, I looked around, but Jax made the decision for me. He pulled me down onto the bed and laid behind me. I expected an arm to come over me, like the old days, but he turned over and slept with his back to me. It wasn't long before I heard his deep breaths and knew he'd fallen asleep. I'm pretty sure I listened to him breathe all night long.

After a day of plotting, we felt ready, and the next evening, Sally's was packed. Again. A pit had been formed around the ring so the throng of drunk people couldn't clamber onto the boxing match. It was for their safety, not the fighters'. The fighters would just punch them and send their bodies soaring back into the crowd.

Surveying the scene from where I'd taken position at one of the ring's corners, I could see my brothers around the bar. Dylan chatted with Haley by the palm tree—still decorated with multicolored thongs and condoms. Dean had taken point at the fire escape this time, and when he met my gaze, he folded his arms over his chest and gave me a disapproving look. It shot right through me, taking me back to when I was six and had strapped firecrackers to his *Sports Illustrated* Swimsuit Edition. I'd thought it hilarious to see little bits of bikini models floating through the air, but he hadn't been amused. And he wasn't now either.

I looked away. I wasn't doing anything wrong. *They* were. But if we explained the situation to them, I knew it wouldn't matter. Not to Dean at least. Dylan would be sympathetic, but our other brothers followed whatever Dean said. And in Dean's mind, this was business as usual. Extenuating circumstances for the jumpers wasn't our headache. That's what he always said. And he had a point. Every jumper had an excuse, a reason why they'd missed court, blah blah blah. Dean had had to stop caring or he'd never take his jumpers in and never get paid.

But this was Jax and this was different.

"Are you ready to get *stuuuuuuunnnng*?"

I narrowed my eyes and stifled a laugh. A yellow jacket mascot now jumped around the ring, pretending to sting people in the crowd. He directed his last taunt my way, his black, beady eyes looking at me almost the same way Dean just had, but he didn't wait for a response. Hopping around to put his rear in my face, he rolled his hips from side to side, wagging the long, black stinger in rhythm with the music blaring from the speakers.

People around me laughed, and when I saw the stinger coming back toward my face, I batted it away. The mascot turned around and huffed, "You don't have to be so violent, woman."

"Get out of my face, you bee-wannabe."

He grumbled, shaking the large yellow jacket head from side to side. "You got no Christmas cheer in you, do you?" Then he laughed, jumped back from me, and raised his black-costumed arms. Striking a pose so his biceps bulged, he rounded his fists toward his head and stuck out his groin. "You know who has Christmas cheer?" He thrust his groin at me again, then turned to the crowd and flung his hands up. *"Do you know who has Christmas cheer?"*

They roared back, *"The Green Jacket does!"*

I rolled my eyes. Jax's opponent called himself the Green Jacket, and because it was Christmas time, he liked to strut around wearing an elf costume. His whole shtick was that he stung like a green jacket, even though his mascot was the yellow jacket. It didn't make sense, but when the Green Jacket came out, no one cared. He was six-foot-two and a solid 250 pounds.

Jax was way leaner. His advantage was his speed, and as I looked around again, I knew we would need that. Three more of my brothers had popped up around the perimeter. And if they were showing themselves, that meant they had other friends positioned all around the bar. Not good. They also liked to keep four outside, just in case. They usually surrounded the place, and I knew they wouldn't abandon that, not with one of their own helping the jumper.

"*God rest ye merry peeeeenis!*" A group of carolers had come in from outside. Two on the end were weaving on their feet, laughing, and the rest of the bar turned toward them. I closed my eyes. A headache formed once again at the base of my skull. I knew where this was going. With the next line, the rest of the bar joined in the song: "*Let anyone…*" The carolers raised their voices. "*…jerk you off!*"

"Oh god," I muttered to myself. This song might never end.

A roar of laughter sounded around the bar, and the carolers kept going. "*Remember to rub and savor. And do it every morn.*"

"Where's your boy?"

I stiffened. Dylan stood right in front of me. Looking past him, I could see Haley still at the condom-decorated palm tree. She lifted her eyebrow and mouthed, "Sorry."

So much for her keeping him busy.

Whatever. I could deal with him. Making sure I wore a guarded mask, I asked, "Who do you mean?"

He snorted, shaking his head. "Come on, you're playing dumb now?"

I waved a hand around. "I'm just sitting here. Enjoying the show."

"*Comfort and joy!*" The crowd was almost screaming the carol now, and they weren't helping my headache at all. Dylan didn't respond, but his shoulders had a settled look to them. When he still didn't reply or move, I had the dreaded feeling he was planning on taking root right next to me.

That wasn't in the plan. I needed him to go away. "What do you want, Dylan?"

"*Wanking it for comfort and joy!*"

His eyebrows furrowed together, and he turned toward the carolers. While his back was turned, I waved at Haley. She lifted her hands in a helpless gesture. I snapped my fingers and pointed at my brother. She mouthed back, "I don't know."

I glared at her, inclining my head forward. She winced and bit on her lip. I wasn't getting help from her. I could see that now.

The mascot came back to us, waving his arms in the air in rhythm with the crowd. He paused in front of Dylan and turned to wave his black stinger in the air, rubbing against the front of Dylan's pants. I waited. This wasn't going to go well, and it didn't take a second swipe before my brother reacted.

His hand shot out and grabbed the stinger. "Buzz off, asshole," he growled. "If you rub that thing against me one more time, I'll drag you into the ring for an impromptu ass-beating."

The mascot looked back. He swung those beady eyes to Dylan, then to me. After a second, he lifted his shoulders in a shrug. "Suit yourself." He moved over, his stinger poised toward me now, and I tensed.

"That's it, you fucker—" Dylan started forward.

"*A blessed angel came, wearing wings and nothing else, brought tidings of glad releases—*" The carolers continued, but a roar came over the crowd, cutting off my brother and their music.

"*Green Jacket! Green Jacket!*" the crowd chanted.

A spotlight went to one of the doorways, and there stood Jax's opponent, striking a pose—similar to the one his mascot had used just a few minutes earlier.

Dylan cursed, skimming the crowd with his eyes. "Where's your boy, Dale?"

The mascot jumped into the ring and began dancing in circles. He waved his arms, sending the crowd into a frenzy.

Holding back a grin, I ignored my brother and turned to watch the Green Jacket instead. He made his way toward the ring, and as he got to us, he grabbed the ropes—and saw the mascot. Pausing, he frowned, but glanced at the crowd. They were clearly loving the mascot, and he shrugged, pulling himself up into the ring.

I hit Dylan's shoulder and pointed to Haley. "You might want to help her." The carolers had stopped singing, and instead, the one closest to Haley was giving her the up-and-down look. He licked his lips, and his eyes darkened.

Dylan groaned. "Where's Jax, Dale?" He started walking backward toward Haley, but he was still waiting for my answer.

I pointed to the mascot. "He's already in the ring. You're too late."

Dylan turned to look, and the announcer started the introductions. "Ladies and gentlemen, your main event! In one corner, at two hundred sixty-three pounds and six feet, two inches with a record of twenty-eight wins and six defeats, heralding from our neighbor Broughten Falls, is the Green Jaaaaaaaacket!"

The announcer pointed, and Jax's opponent went to a corner in his green elf robe. At the end of the introduction, another man removed it and handed it to a group standing outside the ring like I was. The Green Jacket swiveled his head around, a questioning glint in his eyes. The only others in the ring were the announcer, who turned to the corner where I stood, and the mascot, who continued to swing his black stinger at the crowd.

A hip-hop song came over the loud speakers, and the yellow jacket waved his stinger with the beat, pretending to pounce and thrust it out at the crowd, to their continued amusement. Laughter and cheers filled the room.

Then the announcer started again. "And in the other corner, we have our local reigning champion. Weighing in at one hundred seventy-two pounds and standing six feet tall with an impressive record of twenty-four wins and two defeats: Jaxon Cutlerrrrrrrrrrrrrrrrrrrrrrrrr!"

As the announcer finished, the yellow jacket jumped one final time, then reached up and yanked off the mask. A grinning Jax smirked back across the ring at his opponent, whose eyes took on a feral glint. Then Jax turned and looked down at me. I wasn't even trying to hold back my own smirk. The plan had gone off without a hitch. As one, we looked over at Dylan, who'd stopped in the middle of an aisle, halfway back to Haley. His mouth dropped open. Then he snapped it shut and sent me an accusatory look.

I shrugged.

Jax squatted and touched my shoulder. "Part one complete."

I nodded. Part one was getting him in the ring. Part two was his actual fight. My brothers couldn't interrupt it, but he needed to win. Then there was part three: getting him out of the ring and out of the bar without my brothers getting him.

The first bell rang, signaling the fight to start, and I glanced back at Haley. She nodded. She was ready for part three too.

The Green Jacket didn't fare well during the fight with Jax, who looked more like he was getting in a workout than waging a battle. He jumped around his bald opponent, dodging, weaving, doing funky-looking patterns with his feet. At the end of the first round, he dropped to his seat with a wide smile on his face. I didn't have a towel, but I used the arm of the yellow jacket costume to wipe off some of his sweat. The fact that he wasn't sweating much had my competitive side cursing at him and the girl in me swooning. Wrinkling my nose, I pressed the sleeve to the two tiny spots and wiped at some imaginary sweat on his cheek.

"What's wrong?" he asked.

"What?"

He gestured to my nose. "Do I smell?" Lifting an arm, he smelled under his armpit and jerked back, wrinkling his own nose. "Whoa. I don't blame you, but that's from being in there." Tapping the mascot costume, his smile widened even more. "Are you ready for part three, because I'm getting ready to knock this bitch out."

I nodded, gathering the costume together into a ball of cloth. I tried to squish it as small as I could. "Yeah, just wait till it's almost over, though. I need time to get this to Haley."

"Thirty seconds," the ref called out, making sure Jaxon heard him. "Thirty seconds."

Jax nodded at him and looked over my shoulder. "How are you going to get it to her?"

This was the third part of the plan. Haley would wear the yellow jacket mascot costume out of the bar, and because we weren't too original, we were going to use the same ploy as the night before: I'd pull the fire alarm. Jax thought it was genius. My brothers wouldn't expect the same distraction, and anyway, it was the best idea we had.

Sneaking Jax inside with the mascot costume had been the most brilliant point of our plan. I only hoped Haley could get away from my brother long enough to put it on.

"I'm going to the bathroom as soon as you start." I looked over to see Haley resting against the wall, her arms crossed over her chest. When our eyes met, she nodded and glanced sideways to the bathroom.

I closed my eyes in a slow, meaningful manner. I didn't want to nod outright, as my brothers would see that as a signal to someone. To cover up my slow blink, I rubbed at my eye and peeked at Dylan. He was standing in front of Haley, with his back to her. He paid her no attention and glared at us.

"Ten seconds," the ref called.

"You ready?" Jax asked me, standing up.

I nodded. "I'll go drop it off. Give me time to get in my position."

"Time! You ready?" The ref moved to the middle of the ring. He held one hand out between the Green Jacket and Jax, his other keeping his whistle in his mouth. As both fighters nodded, he blew the whistle, sending out a shrill sound that was quickly silenced as the crowd roared.

I hopped off my seat and veered through the crowd. I knew my brothers were waiting for any movement from me, and as I went past Dylan, he caught my hand. "Where are you going?" He wasn't paying attention behind him, and Haley used this to her advantage. Keeping our hands low, I passed the costume to her. She stuffed it in her bag and tapped Dylan on the arm.

He turned to her. "What?"

"I'm going outside. My mom just called me."

"Okay." He turned and asked me again, "Where are you going?"

I pointed to the restroom sign. "I gotta pee."

"Right."

"I do. Stand guard outside, if you want." Instead of waiting for him to release my arm, I twisted it up, forcing his hand to let go. It was either that or it would've broken.

As soon as his hold was gone, I swept into the bathroom. Then I waited to calm down. My heart raced, and adrenaline pumped through me. The fight, sneaking in, and now knowing we'd be sneaking out? All of it mixed together, and I was ready to burst. Pressing a hand to my chest, I took two deep breaths. My heart rate didn't slow, but whatever. My cover wasn't blown, and now it was show time.

I left the bathroom, pausing in the doorway. I needed to wait until Jax saw me. As he did, his mouth curved up, and he ducked to avoid a punch, then brought his left arm up in an uppercut. The Green Jacket fell back two steps, and I started forward. Dylan was there. He reached out to grab me, but I dodged his arm and shoved into the crowd. There were so many people. If I kept my head down, I didn't think he'd be able to track me, and after a little bit, I looked back and saw I was right. Dylan was trying to find me in one direction, so I veered the other way.

The plan after this was more elementary. Haley needed time to get into the costume. I needed time to find a fire alarm, and Jax would finish the fight. Once I found an alarm, I waited. It didn't take long.

The Green Jacket was already sluggish. His foot kept dragging on the floor. I was surprised he'd tired out so quickly, but Jax kept moving around, looking like he was at home horsing around with a friend. He glanced at the crowd for a second, but it was a second too long. I cringed, seeing it unfold.

As Jax turned back, the Green Jacket saw his moment. He flung out a fist and caught him across the face. Jax fell into the ropes, and his opponent was on him, raining punches. Jax frowned and held an arm up to block some of the hits. It wasn't working. The Green Jacket hit him from both sides, and Jax knelt down, cradling his head in his arms to deflect the blows.

I held my breath, but as I continued to watch, I saw the spark of anger appear in Jax's eyes. His jaw hardened, and a mean glint settled in. My heart picked up its pace. This was the Jax I'd fallen for. No matter how he was pushed down, there came a moment when he was done. Every time that line was drawn, Jax came back fighting.

I knew it was coming, but when Jax stood back up, caught his opponent's fist in the air, and reared back to deliver a punch, it didn't matter. The cement wall I'd tried to erect was gone. As he delivered that hit to the Green Jacket, everything I'd been trying to hold back or ignore exploded as well.

I reeled.

So did his opponent.

The crowd went nuts and started chanting Jax's name.

The Green Jacket fell to the ropes, stunned, and Jax didn't waste any more time. He stepped back, then switched his hips and lifted his foot in a perfect roundhouse kick. The back of his heel connected solidly with the Green Jacket's jaw, and his opponent went down with a thud.

He didn't move. It was a knockout win. And that was my signal.

Jax whirled around, and I nodded, reaching up to pull the fire alarm.

The ear-splitting alert sounded, and everyone cursed around me. Jax flashed me a grin, our gazes holding for a moment. My heart swelled, and something else swelled too, but I wasn't going to pay attention to that throb. Then he launched himself over the ropes and began to scurry through the crowd to me.

A second later, I knew he'd been successful. A hand wrapped around my wrist and pulled me down.

"Hi." Jax bent low, keeping his head beneath the crush of people as they streamed past us for the exits.

I grinned at him. "Nice punch."

He shrugged. "He pissed me off. I hope it wasn't too soon, though?"

"Hold on." I stood up just enough to see my brothers peering all around. "I'm not sure." Then I saw her. Haley was doing her best to sneak out with the crowd, and that was the very last signal. I tugged at Jax's arm. "She's there. We have to hurry."

As Haley went past Dylan, Jax and I headed out the other way. I heard a shout over the noise of the crowd, and just before we slipped through the exit door, I stood up and looked back.

Dylan had spotted Haley. He lifted his radio to his mouth, and as one, all my brothers converged. In the next second, Dylan lunged in the air and tackled Haley the yellow jacket, slamming her into the palm tree. It went sideways as both of them fell to the floor. A bunch of condoms rained over them from the tree, and as Dylan reared up to tear off the mascot's head, a green condom fell into his hair. His eyes went wide when he saw it was Haley beneath him, and she smiled, reaching up to pluck the condom off his head. She held it up to him, as if offering a gift.

Jax yanked my wrist and pulled me from the doorway. My brother David ran past me, but it didn't matter. The crowd was our camouflage for the rest of the way, and instead of taking Jax's truck, I pulled out the key to Haley's car. It wasn't long before we drove right past his truck, where two of my brothers were positioned, and out onto the road to drive away.

Jax sighed. "That was awesome."

I nodded, feeling a grin on my face. I had to admit, it was.

CHAPTER
SEVEN

After the fight, Jax informed me he wanted to shower, and to be honest, that was fine because I needed time alone to regroup. The whole night had been one long adrenaline ride, and I was exhausted—though I was still debating whether to fall asleep or jump him and have wild, crazy sex.

When we got to my family's cabin, I was still caught between those two possibilities, so I grabbed a box of wine and headed for the screened-in patio. I was on my second glass when I heard the shower cut off and footsteps leaving the bathroom a moment later.

I held my breath. He was coming my way. Waiting…no, he went into the bedroom. At that image, a whole new fevered rush surged through me: Jax. Bed. Wet. Dripping.

My hand clenched around the wineglass, and I dumped the rest of its contents down my throat. As I leaned forward to fill it right back up again, I reached for the fan on the wall with my other hand. I was hot and bothered. The fan started up on the lowest setting, but that wouldn't do. I switched that thing so it was blowing on high and right in my face.

Then I felt him.

I sat in one of the leather chairs. The doorway was right behind my shoulder, and he didn't say anything. But damn, I could feel his presence.

My blood pumped faster. I needed another fan. I realized I was squeezing my wineglass and forced myself to loosen my grip. I didn't need shattered glass stuck in my hand. Then he'd have to hold it, help me clean the wound, peer close, breathe on it—I sat up straighter in my seat. *Stop thinking, Dale!*

I finally looked up. Yep. He was staring right down at me. I expected a knowing, cocky look, but instead there was something serious in his eyes. He could see right into me.

Fuck. I didn't need that. My loins were already on fire, and that just dumped kerosene on them. My mind began to turn off. I felt myself standing, pushing out of the chair...

Then he said, "Box wine, huh?"

"Yeah." I slumped back down, hoping I'd passed it off as just shifting positions. That word came out like a raspy, garbled moan.

He tossed something in my lap, and I looked down to see a small box wrapped in newspaper with a red ribbon around it. "What's this?"

He moved to sit in the other leather chair. "Something I left here last summer."

Last summer? "You mean..." The night I ended things with him. That night?

He burst into an abrupt laugh. "Yep. *That* night. It was an early birthday present, but everything went to shit, and I forgot it. But now, with all you're doing to help me and in the Christmas spirit..." He lifted a shoulder in a shrug, but looked out toward the lake. "Merry Christmas, Doily."

Shock rendered me speechless for a moment. He'd remembered my birthday. Two months ahead, too. "I'm sorry, Jax."

He waved me off. "Trust me, it's fine. I was an ass most of the time, and I was being one that night too. When you tossed me, that might've been the best thing that could've happened. Losing you was a wake-up call. You ripped my heart out, but thank you for that. I mean it."

Oh god. I had no idea what to say. Then I felt tears threatening to spill, and I shook my head. That'd be more mortifying than anything else. I fanned myself, thinking funny thoughts so I wouldn't cry. *Dylan sacking Haley. Dylan getting sacked in the junk.* That helped a little.

When I knew the tears had stalled, I started. "Jax, that night—"

He held up a hand. "You were right. I was drunk, getting into fights all the time. And that night, I had no right to do what I did."

Oh boy. This conversation had been avoided for a reason. Now I knew it was time. Holy hell. This was going to burn. "You slept with a friend of mine."

"No." He shook his head. Leaning forward, he rested his elbows on his knees, his eyes piercing through the darkness. "I didn't. I'm not lying to you. I really didn't. Susannah told you that, but it was a lie."

"But..." I frowned. "I saw the two of you leave. You were holding hands, and she led you into the woods." I gestured outside. Even though it was dark, I could see the trees in the moonlight. "Right over there. I saw you."

"She kissed me. That was it. I thought it was you holding my hand. Do you remember how drunk I was?"

"But—" Anger crept in. "What happened then, if you didn't sleep with her?"

"Nothing. As soon as she kissed me, I knew it wasn't you. I shoved her away and left."

The whole thing played out in my head again: She'd been holding his hand, leading him into the woods, and Jax had been laughing, but he was talking to his friends. He wasn't looking at her—I hadn't even thought about it. I'd stood there, watching him follow her into the woods, and I saw the outline of them. They were pressed together, and I heard a moan.

I left after that. Too many fights. Jax's reputation was as the best, and I'd grown tired of the guys who always wanted to try to best the best— and the girls. God, the girls. There were so many. I'd fought a lot of them myself. Some of those nights were spent in jail, some weren't, but either way, I was bloody and bruised afterward. Physical pain was always better than the other pain. Always.

I brushed away a tear.

"I came out and saw you leaving," Jax said softly.

I nodded. That was right. He'd found me in the parking lot, even more drunk than I'd been earlier. "I was trying to erase that image of you and her together," I whispered.

"I didn't know you'd seen us. I just saw you leaving."

My hand curled around the present. "What is this?"

He shrugged again, but grimaced. "It's...something I should've given to you anyway. I'm sorry it took so long."

"Jax?"

He cursed and hissed as he flexed his hand. His knuckles were swelling.

"There's an ice pack in the freezer," I murmured, holding the present tight to my chest.

"Yeah." He stood and moved toward the kitchen. Pausing behind me, he touched my shoulder. "I'm sorry for being a dumbass kid for so long. I have changed, despite this weekend. I really have, Dale."

Dale. Not Doily.

My chest swelled with emotion I didn't want to name. I cursed in my head. I shouldn't have helped him. Jax was a weakness of mine. I'd been stupid to think I could guard myself from him.

I heard him in the kitchen and wiped another tear from my eye. But as I opened the gift, I realized I shouldn't have bothered. I took one look at a pendant with a picture of my mother and the birthstone we shared and just lost it. Bending over, clasping the pendant to my heart, I let everything go.

"Hey…" He kneeled beside me. He touched my shoulder and lifted my chin up. "Hey."

I looked at him, but couldn't talk. The tears clogged my throat.

"Oh." He took the pendant and traced his thumb over it. "Yeah, I know how much you still miss her. I'd been messing up so much. I wanted to make it up to you somehow, so I used some of the money I'd won from a fight. I hid it in the bathroom, behind the cupboard's wall. Did you know that's been broken for years? I thought it would've been fixed, but I checked it just now. It wasn't, and this was still there."

The cupboard wall was broken? A chuckle left me. I had no idea. For some reason, the fact that the only one who knew was my ex-boyfriend struck me as hilarious, and I bent over, pealing in laughter.

"Uh…" Jax leaned back. His hand patted my back awkwardly. "Yeah. Imagine that. Still there."

I shook my head, still cackling. He didn't know why I was laughing. I didn't either. Then the tears started again. Sitting back up, I took a few gasping breaths and tried to stop everything: the crying, the laughing, the snort I felt coming. I wiped some of the tears from my face. After my emotions calmed a little, I turned to him with a soft smile. "Thank you."

He grinned. "Yeah." He shifted closer, and his hand lifted to cup the side of my face. "Merry Christmas, Doily."

I groaned. "Why am I starting to enjoy being called that again?" I needed to ignore how his thumb brushed over my cheek. I swallowed a knot and felt the ache forming in the pit of my stomach again.

Nope. It was lower.

Heat surged to my cheeks, but I couldn't turn away. Jax held m hostage with the palm of his hand. His thumb branded me as he continue to rub it back and forth, caressing my cheek.

My god. I still loved him.

That realization exploded inside of me, sending debris everywhere. I was like an earthquake that kept shaking at my core. I started to tremble and when he saw how his touch had affected me, his eyes darkened. The went to my lips, and his hand curved tighter around me, pulling me towar him. He moved closer, and then I felt his breath on me, just beyond touc but so damn close.

This.

This was what my body had been waiting for since I saw him poise to jump out of that window. *Too damn long.* Then my brain switched off. / primal need had built up within me, and it was taking over.

"Dale," he whispered before his lips touched mine.

Holy fuck. He was a drip of water in a desert.

I needed him. I wanted him. I didn't care what happened after this and with that thought—my last rational one of the evening—I whispere back, "Merry fucking Christmas to me."

He chuckled. Then his lips applied pressure, and I was gone.

■■■

When I woke up, my legs wouldn't move. My arms wouldn't move, an yep, I checked—my neck felt like it was sandwiched between two boulders and neither was moving. It was embarrassing that a night of sex could d this to me. I needed to go back to the gym.

A towel landed next to me in bed, and I heard Jax somewhere behin me. "That's your last clean one. If we're staying here tonight, we need t pick up some more from the store."

He sounded cheery.

I wanted to murder him. Instead I yelled, "What did you do to me? can't even move."

The bed dipped with his weight, and he touched my hip. "Yep. Still smooth as silk. What are you talking about?"

"What?" I growled. I wanted to flip over so I could see him, or at least stop him from copping any more feels.

His hand left and returned with a smack. On my ass. "Good bounce there. Still not sure what you're talking about."

Oh god. He was going to continue to grope me until I forced myself to sit up. This was going to hurt. I pushed myself up and around to face him. *That went easier than I thought it would.* Wait, nope. A guttural scream formed as the pain hit me in the next second.

"Oh my god!"

Jax was unfazed. He smirked at me, wearing only his lightweight sweatpants. They rode low on his hips and as he kept grinning, I wanted to curse at him and jump him all over again. Images from the night came to me, helping to ease some of the pain.

Jax had been above me. He'd pinned me down on the bed as he moved inside me. He'd gone slow, purposefully drawing everything out, and watching me the entire time. *Oh yeah.* That memory helped take away a lot of the pain.

Suddenly I was drenched in heat again. Pulling at my shirt, I fanned it around me and looked over the room. Staring at him would only persuade me to pull him back down on top. *Not good.* I couldn't walk after one night. I wouldn't be able to sit if we went another round.

"You're out of shape."

My eyes snapped to his. "Excuse me?"

He laughed, standing from the bed. Raising his arms above his head, he flexed, and as he did, his sweats dropped another inch. I could see the tops of his hips as they molded around his obliques, and if the pants slid another inch down, I'd see him him. Even now, as I stared, a bulge began to grow there.

Jax laughed some more, drawing my gaze back to his. "Keep watching, Doily, and I'll be stripping you naked all over again."

Yes. He had done that too. I tried to snort back. "Whatever. You can think all you want, but..." I stopped talking. He was at full mast now.

His arms dropped, and he came to the bed. Bending down, he rested his arms on both sides of me and leaned over, his face mere inches from mine. His eyes went to my lips.

I couldn't breathe when he was this close. The heat must've been on. *Wait, our cabin doesn't have heat…* "Jax?" What was he going to do? I wanted him to kiss me. His lips were so close.

He leaned back just a few centimeters and trailed his gaze up and down my body. Then he sighed softly. "I want to bend you over, run my hands down your backside, and slide right in," he breathed. "I want to ride you so hard you won't be able to walk for a week, Dale." He closed his eyes and rubbed the side of his cheek against mine.

I gasped at the intimacy, the feel of him there.

He moved again—another sensual graze—and his lips found mine. He kissed me and whispered against my lips, "I want to do so much more than that, and I'm having a hard time convincing myself to walk away and let you be. But if I don't, we'll never leave this cabin. I won't let you go."

Please don't.

His voice was intoxicating. "But I can't do that. I can't miss the fight tonight. You know why?"

I couldn't breathe. I couldn't even try. I just stayed there, feeling his lips on mine. I never wanted to move.

He murmured, "It's because I'm doing the right thing—for my sister and for you, too. I want to do the right thing now, Doily, for you. And I want to continue to do the right thing, for you."

For me. He was doing this for me too.

Fuck that.

I grabbed hold of his sweats and yanked him to me. His lips slammed onto mine, and as our bodies fell back to the bed, he caught himself so he wasn't crushing me. Right before he pushed inside me, I said, "We'll do the right thing in an hour."

Or two.

Or three.

Or after the entire afternoon.

CHAPTER
EIGHT

When we finally made it there that night, as per usual, Sally's was packed. The parking lot was filled, and a crowd waited to get in. We kept driving, but the two parking lots next to it were also full, and in the end, the first spot we found was five blocks away.

We didn't have a genius plan of getting Jax in this time. We'd given everything we had yesterday with the mascot. The only thing I did know to do was ditch Haley's car—and by ditching, I mean I left it in the parking lot of a grocery store a block away from her place. Then I slipped her car keys under her door with a note attached. We hadn't talked for the last two days, so I didn't know the status of her relationship with my brother. I just hoped he didn't see the key first, if he'd slept over. But it wouldn't matter too much. He'd just know we got a new car, which we did.

I'd rented an old-timer's black Camaro. That was all they had at the rental office, and when Jax realized which car was ours, he'd burst out laughing.

"Now that's a ride-in-style kind of car," he said, patting my shoulder. "I'm thinking this is awesome for my last ride to jail tonight."

Ah. Jail. Good times. I needed that reminder of why I was spending all this time with him. Not to jump him—well, not to jump him in *that* way, but in the bail jump kind of way. *Get your head out of the gutter, Doi—Dale. Fuck me.* I shook my head and put a scowl in place. It was time to round third base and head on home.

After parking, we headed down the sidewalk toward Sally's with a crowd. After a couple double takes, Jax cursed softly and reached back to pull up his hood. He stuffed his hands in his pockets and hunched over, trying to look inconspicuous. I rolled my eyes. No matter what he did, he couldn't camouflage his lean build or charismatic presence. He had an almost animalistic draw to him. The people who looked at him hadn't recognized him as the fighter—not yet. They were just drawn to him, as I'd always been. Catching a few seductive looks sent his way, I gritted my teeth. Jax must've sensed my growing irritation because he shot out a hand and caught my arm.

I glanced down at where he'd grabbed me, then realized I'd started moving toward one of the girls. The desire to rip off her arm had been first and foremost in my mind, and when it clicked that I'd been about to do just that, I flushed and pulled back, purposefully moving right next to Jax.

"Who's the fighter tonight?" he asked under his breath.

I sighed. "I know. I know." The old Jax would've let me confront the girl. It was nice to know he really had changed. "Thanks."

He nodded, his eyes going to my lips. "I should get *extra* credit. Watching you initiate a chick fight is the hottest thing I can think of right now." He slid his gaze down my body and back up, lingering on my breasts, then rising to my lips. "Well, maybe not the hottest thing, but you get my drift." He winked at me and bumped his hip into mine. "Don't get me wrong. I'd love for the cops to come and you to join me in jail tonight. The cops love me. I can out-benchpress them. I bet I could get us a shared cell. But you know…" He gestured around the block to where we could see the beginning of Sally's parking lot. "We've got a fight to finish first."

I groaned. "You just ruined it for me. I thought you were a stand-up guy and poof! There went the halo around your head."

He laughed, drawing attention again, so he ducked farther down and quieted. "No halo unless I'm the male equivalent of a Victoria's Secret Angel. Then hell yeah. I'd wear the whole costume. Wings too. They just have to be black. I'm not a white-wing type of angel." He'd gone back to gazing at my lips, and his voice dipped low and promising. "I'm more like a fallen Angel, if you know what I mean."

I did. Too well.

A disturbing tingle filled my body, warming my blood, and swelling my chest with warm fuzzies—the warm fuzzies I still didn't want to deal with because they had nothing to do with our sex-filled afternoon and everything to do with the emotions that continued building in me.

I cleared my throat and pulled my gaze away from his. *Yes.* As soon as I looked away to the growing crowd, I could think better. Then I remembered what we were doing and grasped Jax's arm. "Oh, shit."

"What?" He searched the crowd. "What's wrong?"

"What if my brothers are here? We haven't been looking for them." They could've already spotted us. Glancing around for them, I spotted a familiar face and my heart lurched. It couldn't be...not here...

"Nah." Jax shook his head, pulling me forward. "I talked to one of the guards yesterday. I told him the scoop, and he said he'd sneak us in through the back door."

I shot him a look. The familiar face had disappeared. I was wrong about who I thought I saw. I had to be. "We're bounty hunters. Backdoors are our specialty." Catching the quick smirk on his face, I shot my hand up. "Do not go sexual with that one."

The smirk lessened. "You make it so hard." And the smirk was back.

We weren't going to get anywhere productive with this conversation. "What are we going to do?" I asked. "Just sneak through the crowd?"

"Yep." He pulled me forward into a light jog with him. "Hurry."

Trusting him, I followed his lead, and Jax led me through the parked cars until a big truck passed by. It slowed and began looking for a place to park and deliver its food. Using it as cover, we approached the back of Sally's, hidden from most of the crowd. When it parked, the kitchen door opened, and two guys came out. One was the manager of Sally's. When he recognized Jax, he waved us in. "Turgo's waiting. He'll lead you to the box."

Jax nodded.

The manager eyed me. "The box is for you too. You're his girl, right?"

I stopped, pure panic blasting my insides, but Jax curled an arm around my waist and kept me following him. His mouth pressed in a flat line, and we moved through the kitchen to find a guy the size of a giant wearing a black shirt that said STAFF on it.

"Stop thinking about what he said," Jax whispered under his breath. "We're having fun, right?"

Fun. Right. I bobbed my head up and down.

Jax now asked—I guessed this guy was Turgo—if any of my brother were around, and the security guard/staff member skimmed a hard loo over me, then tipped his head to the side. "We haven't seen any Holder except her in here."

"What about Monroe?"

"Yeah, he's around. He wants to talk to you."

Jax gave me an uneasy look. I agreed, but we'd figured this woul happen.

Turgo stopped talking and waited. Jax gave him a nod, and he led u down another back hallway. When we got to the closed door, Jax opene it and went inside. I got a glimpse of Chris Monroe, but when I starte forward, Turgo stepped in front of me. He folded his arms over his ches "Sorry. He wants Cutler alone."

That didn't sit well with me. "Where's my taser gun when I need i huh?"

He grunted, but didn't seem too worried.

I had no choice. I waited right alongside him.

Jax wasn't long. When he came back out, I straightened from the wal I was about to ask what happened, but I caught his clenched jaw and sti shoulders. He grabbed my arm, pulling me close. Turgo started forwar again, this time leading us out into the main bar area. Jax shook his heac ever so slightly, and I knew he was telling me to wait until we were alone

I did.

Pathways had been cleared through the crowd with ropes on eithe side, and Sally's had been transformed to look like a real boxing venue Turgo led us to our box, and more than a few girls called out to Jax, reachin to touch him. He ignored them, holding me even tighter. His hand presse so firmly into my arm that I knew he would leave a bruise. I didn't te him, though. He didn't know. He was holding onto me for comfort, an that was a good feeling—too good a feeling, to be honest. I should've bee more concerned about how right it felt, but it felt too right for that. I wasn going to fight it.

I still loved Jax. I'd realized it earlier, and I'd slowly started to accer it again.

The rope sectioned off a little sitting area near the ring, and I knew this was the box they'd referred to. Turgo lifted up an end of the rope to let Jax and me through. Once we'd moved inside, he put it back and asked, "Anything to drink or eat? It's on the house."

Jax shook his head and started to sit.

Turgo nodded and turned to leave.

"Wait!" I called. "Water. For him." *Come to think about it...* "I'll take a couple shots, too."

He left, and Jax frowned at me. "I can't take anything. Not right before a match."

I sat and let out a sigh. A knot twisted inside of me. I needed to know what had been said in that back room. "They aren't for you," I told him.

"Oh." He smiled. "Planning on taking me up on that shared cell tonight?"

I fixed him with a pointed stare. "Start talking. What'd Chris say?"

"Nothing about the match. He told me Libby went to see him."

I scooted next to him. "She did?"

A haunted look came to his eyes. "Yeah. She offered to be one of his whores if he'd let her boyfriend off the hook."

My eyes went wide. "What'd he say?"

"No. He held up his end of the deal. He told me to crush my opponent, and he'd do one better: he'd make her boyfriend dump her if he wanted to keep gambling with them. Knowing that dipshit, I bet it'd work too. He'd toss my sister to the curb for the next big game."

I frowned. "He's probably betting on this match with you."

Jax jerked a shoulder up. "I don't care. As long as my sister is out of his life, I'll do what I need to do." He skimmed an eye over me. "You okay?"

I nodded. "Yeah." My fuzzies, butterflies, and twisted pretzel insides were getting along famously. "I'll be fine. So Chris didn't say you had to throw it?"

"No. He said to crush him."

"Oh." That was odd. "Who are you fighting?"

Jax shrugged. "I have no idea. We've been out of the loop. I'll find out when they announce him, I guess."

And that's what happened. Turns out Jax wasn't fighting just another fighter. He was fighting Charles Monroe, Chris Monroe's older brother and also a part of the local Monroe mafia family.

This had just taken an entirely different turn. I shared a worried look with Jax, but when they called for him, he shrugged and said, "I gotta do my job." He rolled his shoulders back, as if shaking off concerns, before jumping from our box and into the ring. As he did, the crowd went nuts.

No matter who won, the crowd had picked their favorite. They loved Jax Cutler.

So did I.

"It's a brilliant idea, isn't it?"

I turned to see Chris Monroe standing in the walkway. Turgo lifted the rope to my box, and Chris ducked under his arm, smiling at me. He indicated Jax's empty seat. "May I?"

I nodded, keeping quiet. Chris Monroe had been in our grade in school. He never said much back then, but everyone knew about his family, so no one messed with him. He'd been the studious type. He was also athletic, but he didn't go out for any of the teams, a fact I've often thought the rest of the guys had to be grateful for. Had he gone out, he would've played, regardless of whether he should've been first string or not.

Looking him over now, I noticed his outfit. He'd worn sweatshirts and jeans in school, never stood out. I always thought that had been his intention—not to stand out—and that sort of still seemed to be the case. Tonight he wore a blue sweater over jeans and loafers. His clothes were high quality, though. He wasn't wearing anything from the local Walmart, unlike 95% of the people in Sally's that night, myself included. I felt a little foolish, knowing I'd bought this shirt from a clearance rack. It'd been so cute.

I didn't feel cute anymore.

"You're supposed to ask what's brilliant," he prompted me, running a hand over his hair. He didn't need to. His brown hair was combed perfectly to the side.

I snorted. "Is this how the mob looks now? The college professor vibe?"

His green eyes seemed startled, then he started laughing, shaking his head. "I forgot you weren't to be messed with."

"I'm a Holden." Holdens didn't get messed with either.

"True." He gestured to the ring where his older brother flexed and stretched, trying to intimidate Jax. "Aren't you going to say anything about that? You know everyone's assuming Jax will throw the match."

I nodded. This was starting to make sense. "And you knew your brother would get to the championship match. All his opponents would throw their fights, not wanting to get on the bad side of a Monroe."

He grinned in approval. "But not Jax."

"Not if he had a good-enough motive."

"Libby." Chris' smile stretched from ear to ear.

"Who you were never going to let pay her boyfriend's gambling debt, were you?" I remembered how he used to watch her in school. When she noticed, he would pretend to be studying. "You always snuck looks at her, thinking no one noticed."

He laughed again, but this time the sound was more somber. "I didn't think anyone did notice."

"You care for her, don't you?"

His smile was gone. He nodded, the somberness moving to his eyes. "I always have."

"Does Jax know?"

"I think he will after this match." He gave me a pointed look.

He was right. I was going to tell. Jax needed to know. "Jax would do anything for his sister."

"I know."

"Everyone's betting on your brother, but your money's on Jax."

He smiled again. "There's a reason why I'm running the family and Charles isn't."

I glanced up at the ring. The announcer was done with the introductions, and he rang the bell, jumping back as the two fighters started to circle each other. Charles outweighed Jax by a hundred pounds. He was solid, and he'd been trained to fight. The Monroes didn't mess around with anything. But Jax was better. I knew it. Jax knew it. Charles knew it, and Chris knew it.

Charles shifted on his heel and threw the first punch.

Jax dodged and came up with an upper cut. Knowing him, he'd want this over as soon as possible, and when he started delivering a series of jabs mixed with roundhouses, the rest of Sally's realized it too. A fresh wave of excitement went through the crowd. Jax wasn't going to throw the match, and as soon as they realized it, they started cheering even louder for him.

Chris was right. It had been a brilliant plan, this whole thing.

"What's the collateral damage from this?" I asked him.

"From Jax beating my brother?"

"Yes."

"Nothing except I get to hold it over Charles for the next ten years."

"Ten years?"

"He's going to prison. This is his last hoorah. The feds got him solid on something, and we can't get him out of it."

I frowned. "So he won't retaliate against Jax?"

"No. I wouldn't let him anyway. I like you and Jax. I always did, even in high school. Jax is one reason why I never went after his sister."

"One reason?"

"Yeah. The other is that I *do* care about her."

After a moment I nodded. He cared enough about her not to pull her into his world. My respect for Chris grew. I didn't know what to say except, "Thank you."

He laughed. "Don't thank me for that. Thank me for keeping your brothers away today."

"What?"

"Dean came to me. They'd figured out why Jax was fighting, and he wanted me to help him bring Jax in. I told him no. I needed my fighter to fight, and I reminded him that you're probably here with the whole purpose of taking Jax to jail tonight." He paused a beat. "You are, right?"

The crowd reached a deafening level. I leaned closer and said, "Yeah. I want to take him in."

"I thought so. There's a car waiting for you after this."

And with that, we heard a thud from the ring. Jax had delivered the last punch. He stood above Charles, who was passed out on the floor: a knockout. Jax whirled around and threw me a grin. The referee called the match and held Jax's arm up in victory. It was done.

Well, almost.

CHAPTER
NINE

We didn't take the ride Chris had offered. Jax insisted on riding in style so we trucked it back toward the rented Camaro. The trip took forever. Without the anxiety of ducking and running from my brothers, Jax was more relaxed, which meant the charismatic Jax came out—or actually that just meant he wasn't holding back or hunching down in his hooded sweatshirt anymore.

The hood went back, and he collected congratulations, fist pumps, and phone numbers left and right as we made our way down the sidewalk outside of Sally's. Getting out of the parking lot was near impossible. A crowd formed around him with more congratulations, and because the doors had been left open, the music spilled out and a dance floor formed right in front of us. People stood on car hoods, sat on trunks, rode on other people's shoulders, and a dance-off soon began. Jax started grinding against me. When people saw that, more drunken guys began thrusting their hips at us, moving in a circle. Jax kept one arm around my waist anchoring me to him. He laughed and was clearly enjoying himself.

Then the shots started coming. A waitress brought a tray of them. Jax said no, but the guys next to him insisted on buying the whole thing. They wanted to drink with the champ. Soon mini cups of Jack, Jim, and Johnny were passed around everywhere. Our town wasn't a big one, so when a local became the champion of the underground fighting ring—and he wasn't a Monroe—it was a big deal.

"Hey!" Haley shoved past a couple of girls trying to get Jax's attention. She gave them a dark look and winked at me.

I waited. She was going to do something.

She did. I watched as she purposefully moved backward into one girl, stepping on her feet. When the girl cried out, Haley whipped around. Her elbow got the other friend, but there were two more girls joining them.

They were busy looking down, patting their breasts and plumping them up, so they didn't see what they were walking into. As they drew closer, the friend Haley had gotten with her elbow stepped into them, bumping heads, and both of them fell back. One tripped and went to the ground. As she did, her skirt bunched up around her waist and left her entire thong exposed—well, not her thong, but everything else: asscheeks galore.

Her friends rushed to block her from view and help her, cursing at Haley, but Haley didn't seem to mind. She drew up next to me with a satisfied smirk. This was how it had been when Jax and I were dating. Oh, I had not missed this.

Jax leaned over, still holding me securely in front of him, and rested his chin on my shoulder.

"Hey, Haley," he said, and a good whiff of liquor came with his words. I wrinkled my nose.

Haley saw my reaction and chuckled again. Reaching into her purse, she took out a mint and held it up for Jax. "Congratulations on the big win."

He took the mint and popped it in, wrapping his arm once again around me. "Thanks. I didn't have to throw it or anything."

"Now you just have to go to jail, huh?" She gave me a look.

"Yeah. I just want to celebrate a little bit," he said. His hand spread out and slipped under my shirt.

Crap. He was drunk. It wasn't illegal for him to be drunk, but it didn't look good.

His fingers began rubbing back and forth over my stomach, and he nuzzled under my ear. One of his fingers dipped down, nestling inside my waistband. My body heat had gone up a notch as he began nibbling my skin, but when his finger dipped into my jeans, a furnace came on full blast. I started fanning myself.

Haley watched all of this with her lips pressed together. She disapproved. I didn't care. I couldn't care. What this man could do with a simple touch was beyond me.

"Yeah, well, now you just have to deal with Dale's family," she told him.

My family. My brothers. Jail.

The reminder cooled me right off, and I gave Haley a thankful look. She harrumphed. "I figured."

She wasn't talking to Jax. That was meant for me, and I knew exactly what she meant. She knew we'd been intimate over the weekend.

I leaned away from Jax's searching mouth. "What? You can't blame me. Hello? You and Dylan. He's my brother."

"I haven't jumped into the sack with your brother," she said. Her cheeks grew pink. "And it's called flirting." She waved a finger at us. Jax caught the tip of my earlobe in his teeth. "That's way beyond flirting, Dale. You can't even lie to me about that."

I snorted. "Not *yet*. You haven't gotten into bed with my brother *yet*." I ignored the rest. Jax now pressed kisses over my cheek, searching for my lips, and I struggled to maintain control.

Haley groaned, pressing her fingers to her temples. "You're right. I'm being all judgey, but seriously, your brothers are coming here. They thought you'd take him straight to jail, and since you haven't, they're coming to do it themselves."

I sighed. One more chase. Then I shook my head. *Fuck it.*

Jax felt my decision as my body tensed, and he lifted his head. His gaze was lidded. "What? What's going on?"

I pulled away, took his hand, and began leading him through the crowd. Haley followed us.

Jax's hands went to my hips. He didn't stop me, he just weaved with me, keeping that intimate hold. When we'd pushed through the main crowd, he leaned forward and asked, "Where are we going?"

"You..." I squeezed one of his hands. "...are going to jail. Then I'll bond you out myself afterward."

He groaned, but didn't fight. "I'm drunk. Jail is very sobering. This is going to suck."

"Yeah, well." I didn't say anything else, but the sooner he got in, the sooner he could get out. That was my way of thinking.

Haley held her hand out. "Give me the keys."

"For what?" She was going to help us? Again?

She lifted her eyebrows. "The keys. What car is it?"

Slowly I took them out of my bag. "You know Dylan's going to get pissed that you're helping."

Haley looked down at the ground, giving me the answer I'd already known: he had been pissed. But she looked back, her chin set firmly. "Give me the keys. They'll know you had to have parked away from Sally's. And someone called and told them they saw you guys walking down Sixth Street, so they're waiting for you. They're going to block you in and make a circle. They figure you can't fight all of them off."

I grunted. Jax was drunk. Who knew what he would do. I didn't relish the idea of him fighting one of my brothers, but I knew the old Jax would've come out swinging if he was cornered. Reluctantly, I put the keys in her hand. "It's the black Camaro parked two blocks up."

"Which one?"

"The only one."

"Oh." She ducked her head. "Got it. Okay. Be back and be ready to jump in Dukes of Hazzard style."

Oh boy.

As she took off, Jax frowned. "Dukes of what?"

I patted his arm. "Just be ready to leap when I tell you."

He nodded. "Got it." A determined look passed over his features, and he lowered his head like a bull ready to charge. "Where do we go?"

"Onward."

We hadn't gotten far when Dylan stepped out from behind a car, stun gun drawn. He wore the whole get-up: his black bulletproof vest with his badge hanging around his neck.

I smirked. "For real? The stun gun?"

He pressed the button, letting the electricity spark, and flashed me a look. "It's up to you. You're going in too, sister."

"For what?"

He gestured to Jax with the stun gun. "Aiding and abetting a criminal, that's what."

Jax looked around. Dylan wasn't alone. Dean brought up the rear, walking right in the middle of the road. He struck an imposing figure since he was three times the size of all of us. The people walking to their cars from Sally's now realized something big was going down. When they saw it involved Jax, they began to shout.

"Shit's going down!"

Someone else yelled, "Pulverize 'em, Cutler."

"You took down Monroe! These guys are nothing."

"Come on, Jax!"

I felt Jax growing tense, pressed up next to me. I glanced down to see his hands in fists and his biceps flexing. He was getting ready to fight.

Oh dear.

Then it got worse. Word must've gotten back to the crowd at Sally's, because a surge of people came sprinting from the parking lot down the block to us. They filled the sidewalks and started banging on the parked cars, slamming fists on hoods and slapping trunks.

"Let's go! Another win, Jax."

No one stepped out onto the street, so it was only Jax and me in the middle. Dean stood at one end, Dylan at the other and then, slowly, the rest of my brothers stepped out from the crowd to close in a circle around us.

David.

Daniel.

Derrick.

Damon.

Darren.

Darius.

I counted. Eight of them. Wait, the last one stepped out and closed the circle right next to Dylan: Deacon.

Jax grunted. "I knew you had a lot of brothers, but they're a little scary when they're all together." He paused and let out a soft laugh. "Especially with you and me being on the other side of things." He touched the back of my arm. "I'm sorry they're being dicks to you."

"I can handle myself," I growled. *They were going to arrest me too? They took out a warrant on their little sister?* The more I thought about it, the angrier I became. That's something we used as a threat, a ploy to get people talking—no one wanted to go to jail. But knowing they'd actually followed through and gotten a warrant on me? That was low.

I was going to bust my brothers up. "I could really use my Taser right about now…"

Jax cracked his knuckles. "No need, Doily. Let me handle this."

"Wha—" He wasn't going to take them all on….was he?

Nope. Jax was looking past my brothers to where a set of headlights bore down on them, coming fast. When Dylan didn't seem to hear the car behind him, Jax shouted, "Watch out!"

Dylan, Deacon, and Damon all looked back at the same time, and they saw the same thing I did: my rented Camaro soaring right at them. The bass was going, and the engine revved.

Haley had really meant it about the the Dukes of Hazzard entry, and I turned to warn Jax, but I didn't need to. He wrapped an arm around my waist as my brothers scattered, and the Camaro barreled toward us. Haley slowed down just enough for us to see both side doors open and ready. Jax threw me into the backseat, and as soon as his hands left my waist, he leapt for the front seat, slamming the door shut.

"*Go!*" I yelled, holding on to a seatbelt, and Haley jerked the tires around. There was enough room, just barely, for her to do a complete 180. Dylan and two of my other brothers had started into the street, but when they saw the Camaro coming back, they leaped out of the way again, and we sailed right past them.

I wound my window open and yelled Dylan's name. When he looked up, I extended my middle finger. For good measure, I lifted my arm as high as I could and hollered, "Merry Christmas to you, too!"

Haley laughed as I pulled my arm back in. She slowed at the stoplight and turned right to travel to the police station. "That was the most dramatic escape ever to only go a few blocks, but it was awesome. I think your brothers are more pissed that they got outwitted by their little sister than anything else."

"Male egos."

"Hey." Jax turned around. "Why do I feel like that was an insult?"

"Because it was." I gave him a grin. "But you're exempt. For a guy who should have an ego, you don't."

He laughed, turning back around. "I've messed up too much to get a big head." He patted the dashboard. "Take us to jail, Haley. It's a good day to wear orange."

She barked out a laugh. "I don't think you'll have to wear orange. You shouldn't be in there too long."

And she was right. Once inside, Jax and I together, holding hands, found out all charges had been dropped against him. The assault on his sister's boyfriend lacked enough evidence to prosecute. Apparently, the boyfriend had come in to the station earlier, escorted by guys known to work for the Monroe family, and he'd recanted everything. It had all been a big misunderstanding. His bruises were from a fall down the stairs, and Jax had only talked to him. Never touched him.

There were no witnesses to corroborate his initial statement, so the clerk told Jax he was free to go. As for me, there was now no criminal for me to aid and abet, so that meant I hadn't broken a law either.

It happened so fast that Haley was still in the parking lot when we went back outside. She'd just started to pull out, but she saw us and hit the brakes. Turning the car off, she got out and waited for us to come to her. "What happened?"

When we told her, she burst out laughing. "That must've all happened today. God, that's going to piss off your brothers even more." She held a hand up. "Please, please, please, let me be the one to tell Dylan. I constantly want to jump him like I have ants in my pants, but he's just delicious when he's pissed off. I think I like pissing him off the most."

"Sure." I couldn't contain my smile. "Have at it."

As if on command, my brothers' black SUVs pulled into the station parking lot. There were four in total, and Haley took her time sauntering over to the one Dylan drove. She made sure to sway her hips from side to side.

I started toward Dean, but Jax drew me back.

"What?" I asked.

"Just a minute."

"For what?"

He slid a finger under my chin, lifting my head until our eyes met. "What's going to happen with us now?"

"What do you mean?"

"You and me." An unsure look flashed across his face. He tried to hide it, but I saw.

I melted. I'd been angry at my brothers, but now, with that one look, I was a mess once more. I squeezed his hand and lifted my lips to his. He frowned and asked against my mouth, "Does this mean what I think it means?"

Curling a hand up and around his neck, I grabbed hold of his hair and whispered, "You're goddamn right it does." Then I pulled him down and kissed him. I didn't care about my brothers' reactions. I didn't care about college. I just didn't care.

I was still in love with Jax, and I wasn't letting him go. Not again.

Happy holidays to me.

AUTHOR NOTE

For more stories like *Fighter,* go to www.tijansbooks.com.

CPSIA information can be obtained
at www.ICGtesting.com
Printed in the USA
BVHW060224280122
627358BV00012B/1109